VHAIDRA & [illegible] DESTINY OF NIKODEMOS

NICHOLAS STANOSHECK

No.8, 3rd Cross Street,
CIT Colony, Mylapore,
Chennai, Tamil Nadu – 600004

First Published by Notion Press 2020

ISBN 978-1-7349140-0-9

This a work of fiction. Names, characters, businesses, places, events, locales, and incidents are either the products of the author's imagination or used in a fictitious manner.
Any resemblance to actual persons, living or dead, or actual events is purely coincidental.

E-Book Edition ISBN: 978-1-7349140-1-6
Library of Congress Control Number: 2020906599
LCCN Imprint Name: Dallas, Texas
Publisher: Notion Press
Cover Design: Stan Saint Yak
Editor: Obed Joshua
The following Adobe Fonts are licensed for personal & commercial use and were used in this publication:
IM Fell Great Primer © Igino Marini, IM Fell
Modesto Condensed © Jim Parkinson, Parkinson Type Design

DEDICATION

To Keith Penewit, who introduced me to the world of medieval fantasy adventures.

To Ann Fornoff, who challenged and inspired me to write with passion and heart.

CONTENTS

PROLOGUE
BEFORE IT ALL BEGINS

Hypodiakonos Nikodemos, known as 'Demos' to his friends, was a hypodiakonos of The Way, the religion that worshipped The Ancient of Days, a triune God, also known as the Creator-Logos-Ghost. Demos had long, black hair and a long, black beard. He was fat, as he loved to eat food as well as drink beer and wine.

As a Cleric of The Ancient of Days, he could do healing chants. He was a *third rank* Cleric of The Way, so his healing was at about the same level as a healing potion. His goal was to one day, through study and experience, be able to raise the dead to life, as the elderly clerics of his faith could do.

His *episkopos* wanted him to become a cleric-monk, to join the local monastery and eventually, become an *ieromonk*, but Demos was insistent that he wanted to marry instead. He had not found any-one of his faith to marry yet, but he was still sure that he wanted to marry, once he found the right lady. His episkopos agreed to wait to ordain him a *diakonos* and then, a *presbyteros* until after he married a woman of

The Way who was willing to become a *diakonissa* and *presvytera*.

Today was his thirty-third birthday. So, after serving at the *Kyriaki Liturgy*, and having a great feast with friends, he returned home to the land that he owned, and there, while in prayer, he felt a supernatural call to go hunting in the nearby forest.

He put on his chainmail armour under his white robe, a black vest, and a skufiya hat. He grabbed his beloved Yan Yue Dao weapon, named *Qing Long*, which had a bone blade and wooden handle with enchanted green *jade* dragons decorated all over it. He had got it as a gift when he was younger, doing missionary work in the mysterious land of *Zhong*. He loved to use this weapon for hunting and was fierce and fast at chopping an animal's head off.

As he walked from his city of *Sicyon*, past the beautiful Estate known as *Omorfia Dipla Sto Potami*, he did prayers on his prayer rope, called a *chotki*. He had completed almost one hundred prayers when he heard screams of a female followed by aggressive laughter by multiple males. The Ancient of Days had sent him here to save someone; he was sure. He ran to the sounds to serve justice!

Vhaidra was a *drow* monk. The drow were a race of subterranean *dark elves* with grey to almost black skin, white or silver hair, and were born with red, violet, yellow, or on rare occasions, green eyes. They, as a rule, worshipped an evil Goddess known most frequently as the *Dark Mother* or the *Spider Queen* and killed without any care. Their underground homes were in subterranean tunnels that they called *the underworld.* They were a murderous, hateful race, except for a few rare drow who found the whole concept of the Spider Queen's chaotic and evil society to be both sick and pointless.

Vhaidra was one of these rare drow. Because of this, she had removed the spider and web motifs from her leather and bone armour and made one of her own design, much to the chagrin of her latest *archimandrite.* She was a monk and had lived in various monasteries. There, she had learned how to kill or disable prey and foes with her hands, head, and feet. She also was an expert with her unbreakable lightning-infused bone staff and her poison-dipped throwing daggers, which were also made of bone.

Drow society was matriarchal, and there was a strict order of power among the *houses* according to the Dark Mother's favour. Often, one 'lesser' house would attack a 'greater' house, killing all of its members, and would take that house's place in the hierarchy.

This happened to her house, and a house servant was sent to Vhaidra, requesting her to leave her monastery and come help stave off the attack by such a lesser house. She was quick to accept, but when her archimandrite refused to let her leave, she snapped and killed the head of her monastery. This caused the other three monks of the monastery to attack her, and Vhaidra would have to kill all of her fellow monastics to escape and help her house.

In the process of this battle, one of the other monks, Myronia, had grabbed her unbreakable bone staff and used a chant to hide it far, far, away in the underworld. While Vhaidra did not necessarily enjoy killing all of her fellow monks in her monastery, killing Myronia brought great joy to her.

Once she had escaped the monastery, alive, but beaten down, she headed to her house, which looked much like a giant castle, and she found it ablaze. Six members of her house were trying to escape, and so, she helped lead them to escape to the surface.

Once they got there, they found the light in the forest to be blinding. Vhaidra had thankfully practised *bright light training* in the monastery, where she trained in full light, which prepared her for being in the *overworld.* Unfortunately, the tunnel that led them to the overworld put them amid seven *high elves,* mortal enemies of the drow. Vhaidra told her sistren and brethren what to do, and by the time she had killed four of the high elves with her throwing daggers and via hand-to-hand combat, she found that all from her house had run away like cowards, rather than help her fight off the high elves.

"By the Dark Mother! I risk my life by fighting my way out of the monastery and saving what is left of my house, and I am betrayed and left for dead like this?" she muttered to herself.

Unfortunately, her adrenaline was leaving her after hours of fighting and running, and she was knocked hard to the ground, which caused her to uncontrollably scream out in pain, yet unable to move.

Elder Dionysios was the *Guardian of the Armour of The Ancient of Days* in Sicyon. He was a revered hermit who lived in a catacomb cell. He would pray fourteen hours a day, eating only raw nuts, fruits, and vegetables brought to him by followers of The Way. He studied the Will of his God eight hours a day, which empowered him to do sorcery that some called miracles, like calling down the *Uncreated Light*, causing storms, transforming water to blood, creating earthquakes, calling on plagues of locusts or serpents, making crops grow, healing the sick, raising the dead, etc. He only slept two hours a night. He was waiting for the day that The Ancient of Days would choose a *chosen*, the one that would wear the Armour permanently. Elder Dionysios was destined to be both the Guardian of the Armour and the adviser to that monk.

Ti'erra was a *half-elf* dancer who danced in the bar called *Brother*, run by the *Jet Fist Gang* in Sicyon.

She had a *greathammer* that she could swing around gracefully while she danced and in combat, but currently, she used it as a dancing pole, placing the stone hammerhead on the ground and then swung around on the wooden handle in various forms of undress. Her speciality was hooking her foot in the leather handle at the base of the greathammer and swinging around naked. The dance, along with her low-level Elven magicks that charmed others, creating a greater level of attraction, always earned her lots of tips.

Miriam had recently lost her baby upon his birth. Distraught, but wanting to help children with no mothers, she volunteered as a milkmaid at her local monastery orphanage in *Halab*, far away from Sicyon. She also taught the older children archery, as she had been an expert archer in her youth, and had found that it helped her to learn to focus on her goals.

CHAPTER I
THE BEGINNING

Vhaidra could remember that first year as if it were yesterday...

DAY 1

She was lying there, abandoned by her fellow drow of her house. The high elves attacked her fiercely. She knew she would die at any moment. In defiance, she kept her eyes open, staring angrily at these high elves, showing no fear, and tried not to flinch as she was brutally attacked.

In the distance, she heard a low voice yell out, "Hey you, stinkin' heretic elves, leave her alone!"

With the bright light of the overworld and blood running into her eyes, she could barely make out the hulking human with what appeared to be a big staff. He was spinning his weapon and charging the overworld elves, telling them to leave her alone the whole time.

This did not stop the high elves until he placed his body between her and them. Then, they simply turned their rage onto him and attacked him fiercely. He took on damage, protecting her while blocking their attacks, and used his staff to ward them off.

It seemed like it took forever, but eventually, the high elves were beat down. The human checked on her, but the last thing she said, speaking in the Drow language, before losing consciousness was, "*Sevir uns'aa ulu el, Rivvil!*" which meant, "Leave me to die, human!"

DAY 8

She awoke, unbeknownst to her, an entire week later. The human was tending her wounds, anointing them with oil. In the low light, it became clear now that he was a cleric of some sort and had some wounds on his face and hands from the battle with the high elves. Another bearded cleric, vested in gold, who was the older of the two humans, was holding a holy book and chanting words. A younger human, an acolyte, also vested in gold clerical garb, was holding a large golden candle and a golden censer, burning incense.

After the chanting was completed, her rescuer kissed the hand of the Elder Cleric, who then left with the younger human acolyte. Vhaidra reached out and grabbed his hand, making it bleed with her razor-sharp nails and asked, "*Vel'uss ph'dos, lu'ele xunus dos dormagyn uns'aa?*" which translated was as, "Who are you and why did you save me?"

"Oh... you... awake!" replied her rescuer in a very broken attempt to speak in one of her many known languages, "I... be... Hypo... Diak... onos... Niko... Demos... who... be... you?"

She was shocked that this human could speak the common language of the underworld.

She replied, "I am Vhaidra of the House Ou... of the... of ... of no house," she paused, lowering her head and taking deep breaths, and continued, "By the Dark Mother, why did you save me?"

"Three... bigger... male... heretic... high... elves... attack... one... smaller... female... elf... hate... crime... can... not... allow," he replied.

Vhaidra did not understand. Why did this human speak the common language of the underworld? Why did she call the high elves heretics? Why would this human seek justice against high elves in a war that he was not involved in? Why would he side with a Drow? Humans usually were allies with the high elves (even though those same elves looked down on humans as inferior creatures) along with the *wood elves* of the overworld. So, they fought against drow.

"Thank you, Hypo," she said as she let go of his hand, closed her eyes, and went back into an extended elven reverie. He chanted healing prayers from his holy book for her.

DAY 40

That was then; this was now. Hypo, as she called him, cared for her, helped heal her by use of herbs, oils, and rituals for another month. She remained puzzled for a long time about why this human Cleric had helped her. She made sure to watch him carefully and learn everything about him so that she could understand. Vhaidra did not like not being unable to understand anything in her surroundings. Because of this, she focused on mastering the overworld human's language, a language she knew bits of since her youth for strategic purposes.

Hypo was the opposite of what was seen as an ideal male in the underworld of the drow. He was thirty three years old, blue-eyed, tall at five feet and nine inches, fat at two hundred twenty pounds, had thick black hair pulled back in a ponytail (and his hair was not just on his head but on thick black hair on his face and a light layer all over his body!), and worried himself about peace and justice. He wore a flowing white robe with a black rope belt and a black vest with many pockets over it. Inside his robes, he wore light chainmail armour. He wore a necklace with the symbol of his God on it, but he oddly always wore it inside his robe.

Vhaidra was a typical drow monk, smaller and thinner than overworld elves such as the wood elves and high elves. She was cold as ice, three hundred and twenty one years old, chartreuse-eyed (a colour that few dared to call green) short at four feet and eleven inches tall, muscular but thin and light at ninety-nine pounds, small breasted with a high, round forehead and buttocks, had long white hair (and like all elves, she only had hair on her head, eyebrows, and eyelashes) which she wore in two tall pigtails that came down towards her ankles before curling back up. Her ponytails could be used as powerful whips themselves. Her long sideburn hair hung down past her waist as well. She worried herself about power and revenge, which was justice to her. She wore armour made of strong, yet lightweight *black leather* and *bone*, including horns and teeth from fierce underworld monsters. Her armour included thigh-high black leather boots with horns at the knees, heels, and toes. She had bicep-high tall gloves that had horns at the elbows and sharp, pointed teeth at each finger's topmost knuckles. Her leather skirt was of medium length, and her black leather corset top had large shoulder pads with three large horns on each shoulder, attached to the thick straps. She wore enchanted magenta *jacinth* amulets encrusted in bone that strengthened her armour, and gave her *fire protection* on her wrists, ankles, in her large belt, her choker necklace, and her circlet. Her black leather bands that held up her large twin pigtails were also encrusted with these enchanted jacinth stones.

Many dark elves could not use their spells in the overworld, as it was magick tied to either the worship of the Spider Queen or to the underworld itself. As a monk, Vhaidra's spell-casting was tied to her *qi*, so that she could use her various chanting spells anywhere without difficulties. With her qi, she could call for a solid black cloud of complete *darkness* or a cloud of powerful *acid* that was the same chartreuse colour as her eyes. In addition to this, Vhaidra could raise and command the skeletons of fallen warriors and beasts to fight by her side.

One thing that Vhaidra liked immediately about this human was that he carried an image with him and kissed it often when saying his prayers. He called it an *Icon of the Most Holy Theotokos*, and she was the mother of his God. His God, interestingly called The Ancient of Days, was only a child in the image.

This God-Mother was obviously a queen, and she bore the wounds of an attack. Anti-Devils, called angels, held her crown in place on her head. She was dark-skinned, unlike the much lighter-skinned Hypo.

She realised that this human's veneration had no bearing on race or sex. This had helped her to start to understand and appreciate her rescuer.

After a month, Vhaidra was able to walk unassisted and had mastered a lot of the common human language, which she had learned somewhat during her education in the monasteries. Being a fast learner, she was almost fluent, although she had a thick accent. She was ready to leave the city and was ready for adventures as she discovered her new life above the underground. City life in the overworld was acceptable, but she desired more from her life.

She told Hypo that she wanted to go on exciting journeys and use her martial warfare skills which she had honed in the monasteries of the underworld. Hypo told her that if she wanted to do this, he would go with her for her protection. She explained that she no longer needed his protection, even with all the racist overworlders she had encountered, but he still wanted to go, and she obliged his request.

Hypo suggested that they go to a dungeon at the nearby city of Corinth and slay a small red dragon that he had heard was harassing the local citizenry.

Vhaidra no longer had a house of her own. She was a monk who no longer had a monastery, an archimandrite, or even a Goddess or God. She wished she could find one other than the evil Dark Mother. She had long ago questioned allegiance to the masochist Goddess, the Spider Queen, and had since been betrayed by her house and abandoned, left to die. She wondered if her lack of faith and a curse of the Dark Mother had been the direct cause of this series of events.

If it were not for Hypo, she surely would be dead, being tortured in the afterlife's *shades* by the Goddess' demonic minions. For now, somehow, she belonged in the overworld, where there was actually a selfless being, a human of all things, who she could trust, and who she called Hypo. This would be her home, until one day, at last, she could have her revenge on the usurper house in the underworld. However, she knew very well that revenge was a dish best served cold.

DAY 41

Before they left Sicyon, she attended her rescuer's Kyriaki Liturgy, one of his religious rituals held in the local Temple of The Way. She stood in the back of the temple and just observed. When she entered, Hypo got her one of the hooded capes that females could borrow for wearing during the Liturgy. Wisely, he chose a black silk one with magenta trim. He explained that all women in the temple wore these blessed capes during prayers to ward off the demons. She didn't think she needed any such protection as she had fought demons with her qi in the past, but she did not protest his actions. The others in attendance greeted her kindly, something she would not often find elsewhere in the overworld. After the ritual, there was a shared *agape* meal, which acted as their pre-adventure breakfast feast. She did not care much for the meal, but bit her tongue, and did not complain.

As the pair left for adventures, Vhaidra realised that it was not a large staff that Hypo carried, as she had previously thought, but it was rather what he called Qing Long – a type of halberd from the Far East land of Zhong. The people of Zhong called it a Yan Yue Dao. She had never seen a weapon like this before! It had a large crescent moon blade made of bone at the top, and the handle was covered in jade green dragons. With this enchanted weapon, he could attack from as far as seven feet away and inflict acid damage. He also carried healing oils, holy salt, and holy water that would damage and scare some creatures.

She, on the other hand, preferred her spells and poison-dipped throwing daggers. She could throw three from each hand at a time. These enchanted daggers could easily fly over 100 yards through the air to the heart of her enemies. She also liked to use her close-up weapons of horn-armoured feet and her teeth-armoured knuckles. Once upon a time, she had used an unbreakable bone staff, but that had been stolen and hidden away from her with powerful magicks.

Their travels took them south and then east, where they would enter a dungeon facing west.

Before they entered their first dungeon, Hypo stopped Vhaidra and performed a ritual, praying to his God and asking him to protect them both. Then, he kissed his icon. Vhaidra appreciated the gesture, but she knew that survival was ultimately up to the two of them, not up to any Gods or Goddesses.

Hypo lit the candle in his lantern and went into the dungeon. Vhaidra scurried along the shadows since she could see perfectly in the dark. Inside, they would venture to find the red dragon which was attacking the local populace.

Vhaidra shouted out from the shadows, "Gelatinous Cube!" She began to raise a skeleton to temporary life from the bones of previous adventurers who had not survived their journey into this dungeon. Hypo pulled out his Yan Yue Dao named Qing Long and started spinning it.

Vhaidra's mindless skeleton was not skilled in tactics, but from behind, it hacked at the cube with its only possession, a short sword. Thankfully, the gelatinous cube was also mindless and did not turn its course. Hypo brilliantly spun and chopped pieces from the cube. Vhaidra could do nothing but watch. She knew her throwing daggers were of no use and hand-to-hand combat with a gelatinous cube was impossible and suicidal.

Once the gelatinous cube got down to a manageable size, Vhaidra's skeleton fell into it and was consumed. Hypo, exhausted from his battle tactics, reached into one of his pockets and pulled out a bag. He reached in, pulling out his blessed salt, and threw it in a cruciform pattern while saying a prayer. The gelatinous cube squealed a horrifying sound and shrunk into nothingness.

On the ground were some trinkets which the duo collected before moving on to where they would stop for a light lunch.

"By the Dark Mother, that was impressive, Hypo."

"Thank The Ancient of Days, not the Dark Mother, that it was impressive, Vhaidra." he retorted, "Why didn't you attack the gelatinous cube directly?"

"Hand-to-hand combat with a gelatinous cube is stupid, and if I used poison daggers, the gelatinous cube would have been poisonous, possibly poisoning you."

"That's what I thought, but I wanted to make sure," Hypo replied with a wink. "I loved that mindless skeleton trick. How many can you raise at a time?"

"Only one at a time, but if I have the time and energy, I can raise up to five in a battle. Rarely do I have that type of time while being attacked. Plus, sometimes, they attack each other by mistake."

"Too funny!"

"Not very funny in a life or death situation," she bluntly explained.

"I guess not. Let's eat."

"Affirmative," she replied, hoping that this meal would be better than the agape meal they had that morning.

Thankfully, for her, once he broke out their rations, she quite enjoyed this meal of dried meats and fruits better than their previous agape meal that was full of grains and dairy products that were barely palatable to her.

After dinner, they entered into a huge, well-lit area of the dungeon where wooden supports held up the stone walls and ceiling. A large smokeless fire was burning in the middle of the room. Skeletons littered the floor all over this area. Once inside, they ran into a group of three *sylvans* or wood elves, who immediately pulled their bows out and attacked the pair. Nikodemos was surprised that the sylvans attacked them so quickly without any provocation at all. He swung Qing Long and destroyed all six of the arrows that they had fired at Vhaidra. The trio then turned both their attention and their bows towards the human. He was instantly pinned against the wall by the quiver-full of arrows and was unable to free himself.

Vhaidra cast a darkness spell to engulf the three wood elves and then, threw six poison daggers. Hiding in the shadows as much as possible, she started to raise a skeleton. Thankfully for her, the sylvans were confused in the pure darkness, which was darker than the dark in which they, like elves, could see in, and were all poisoned. Before her skeleton advanced, she threw six more poison-coated daggers. Then, she raised one more skeleton before deciding to save the Cleric.

She ran over to check on him. He had arrows through one arm and one leg, but other arrows had pinned him to the wooden supports via his heavy robe. She pulled the arrows that had pierced him out of the wood, cutting the tips off, but left the shafts inside Hypo. He collapsed, unable to hold himself up on the wounded leg.

Vhaidra threw six more poison-laced daggers and raised the third skeleton. As the darkness faded from her first spell, she cast one more darkness spell and engulfed the three sylvans and three skeletons. Once again, she threw six more poison daggers and then, pulled the heavy Hypo to the shadows, where they rested.

Hypo put a piece of cloth into his mouth and pulled two arrows out of his arm and three arrows in his leg. Blood poured out, and he took cloth strips to bind the wounds.

The darkness spell lifted, and Vhaidra could see that all that remained were two of her skeletons, who were fighting each other. The wood elves had been hacked by her skeletons. The sylvans had shot each other in confusion and were poisoned from multiple dagger wounds.

Once her skeletons had killed each other, Vhaidra went and beat up the corpses, letting out her rage. Then, she collected the treasure, leaving the studded leather armour, and breaking the long-range weapons on her dead foes. She also collected some of the sylvans' medical supplies, scrolls, and healing potions. She then brought them all back to Hypo.

She took off his bandages, washed his wounds with the holy water that he had brought, anointed the wounds with his holy oil, and re-bandaged him. She heard him chanting and saw him holding his icon while she did this. She gave him the powerful sylvan healing potion to drink.

Vhaidra set up camp and prepared a light dinner meal. Hypo took off his belt, vest, and chainmail, lying down on his bedroll to sleep wearing his robe. He drank more of the powerful sylvan healing potions, read his evening prayers, and fell asleep, snoring loudly.

The drow pulled out the scrolls she had collected from the wood elves and read them. From it, she realised that the sylvan rangers had been hired by the high elves who had almost killed her when she was escaping the underworld. She didn't understand why this was happening, but she would find out later and kill the high elves who had escaped her attacks before. She started to wonder if these high elves had been hired by her drow enemies.

Vhaidra stayed up for another hour, searching around the campsite, making sure the walls were clear. She also checked for traps on the floors. The fire prevented her from properly seeing the ceiling. She threw the bodies of the sylvans on to their bonfire and let them burn. Once the flesh was fully burned, she reincarnated a wood elf skeleton to have it stand watch while they rested.

She did not take off her leather and bone armour, as she rarely did so, except to clean it, but lay down next to Hypo with her back to his stomach, so she could easily attack while protecting him in case of a midnight ambush. She could not believe how much heat he radiated but enjoyed the seemingly magickal aura of warmth that helped her relax. There was something that she found comforting about this. She smiled, closed her eyes, and slipped into her elven reverie.

DAY 42

Four hours later, she woke up and was surprised to find herself being held by the human. Although shocked, she found deep satisfaction in the fact that during the night, he had actually draped his arm over her. It almost seemed that he held her close to him to protect her. After an hour, she slipped away from his comfortable and warm embrace and checked the area again before preparing their breakfast.

Hypo awoke in a lot of pain. "Ow. Hey! What is that smell?" he asked Vhaidra.

"Oh, it must be the sylvans."

"Oh, I was afraid it was breakfast. Do they normally stink that badly when they die?"

"Only when I burn their bodies!" she laughed.

"Wait, we aren't having sylvans for breakfast, are we?" Hypo asked.

With a great big grin on her face and giggling at the idea, Vhaidra replied, "No, they were full of poison. We're having the sylvans' rations that they had in their packs."

"Good! From what I hear, elves really know how to cook!"

"Some do, some don't. I guess you'll find out if they do!"

After his morning prayers, they ate. Vhaidra washed and anointed Hypo's wounds again, binding them tightly. She helped him get dressed and use Qing Long as a crutch so that he could walk without putting pressure on his wounded leg. Hypo looked up, gasped, sighed, and finally, looked down at the ground.

"What is it?" Vhaidra asked.

"Well, I guess we are even now," he replied, looking at the ground.

"What do you mean?"

"I saved you from three elves and healed you, and now, you have saved me from three elves and healed me."

"I wasn't even thinking that..." she replied, growing angry, "I didn't know that you thought that I owed you!"

"Well, since we are even, I will bid you adieu and go back home. Bye, Vhaidra!"

With that, he turned back to the way they had entered and hobbled away. Vhaidra could feel her blood pressure rising. He had just turned his back on her! She actually started trusting someone for the first time in ages and this human overworlder turned his back on her! Did he only care about being owed something this whole time? She screamed in anger and pulled out six throwing daggers. She was getting ready to throw them at Hypo in a rage when she heard a sound of six feet hitting the ground.

It was the high elves; the very same three high elves from who Hypo had saved her – the high elves who had hired the wood elf rangers to kill them. Apparently, they had been slowly crawling down from above and then dropped down, surrounding her. She was unaware of this tunnel above this room, as the bright light of the bonfire had blinded her from seeing this.

One of the high elves hissed at her, "This time you will die, Drow!"

She was surprised but jumped to the occasion. She threw her previously prepared throwing daggers as she initiated a darkness spell to surround all three of them along with herself with pitch-black darkness. Being able to see in the dark, including extreme darkness spells, she whisked away to where she had burned the sylvans the night before. There, she used her strength to raise one wood elf skeleton after the other until all three were raised and were shooting arrows at the high elves. She heard the rangers' arrows bouncing off of the plate armour of the high elves, but was hopeful that the sheer number of arrows would mean that some would hit them in between the plates or in their exposed faces.

Vhaidra launched another darkness spell to keep them in the dark and started to hear something weird. It was the screaming of the high elves and the sound of bone cutting through metal. This only lasted a few minutes, but then, there was silence. Her skeletons were still shooting, and she heard a voice call out in a broken attempt at the underworld language, "Make... skeletons... cease!"

She reached out and twisted the skulls off her skeletons, making them collapse into a heap of bones. Once her darkness lifted, she saw Hypo with arrows in his arms, lying on the floor with a bloody Yan Yue Dao along with three Elven shields and swords. She also saw that the three high elves were cut into many pieces.

"You came back!" she exclaimed, admittedly confused.

"I never intended to leave you, Vhaidra! I saw the high elves descending from above and knew the only way for us to take them out was by surprise. So, I pretended to abandon you, so that you might be angered enough to take your weapons out and then, I could secretly attack them from behind."

"So, this wasn't all about me owing you?" she asked in a low voice.

"Never! After all, I'm not yet healed," he said with a wink. "Really, you don't owe me anything. It was my great honour to rescue you!"

Vhaidra ran over, kicked the heads of the dead high elves, and then, helped him back up after removing the arrows.

"I can't go on to the red dragon Vhaidra, do you want to accompany me back to Corinth and Sicyon to find an *apothecary* and to call upon the episkopos?"

"I wouldn't have it any other way," she replied, and helped him out of the dungeon with a smile, "We will simply have to return to this adventure at a later date when you are all healed. This time, it will be my turn to care for you, clean your wounds, anoint you with oil, brush your hair, and have prayers read over you, as you once did for me."

"Thank you, Vhaidra. You are the best thing to have happened to me this year."

Vhaidra smiled, cried one solitary tear, being touched by authentic kindness that she had never experienced before, and inaudibly replied, "Me too, Hypo, me too."

CHAPTER II
BEGIN AGAIN?

DAY 50

The strong medicine the apothecaries had given Nikodemos had knocked him out. When he came to, he smelled something wonderful and found that Vhaidra had cut his hair to a short spiky style and was shaving his beard while singing a drow hymn,

"Dos phu'morfel d'orbb's solen
Dos phu'morfel verin
Vel'klar ussta ssinssrigg unl'r
Lu'dosst ssinssrigg kre'jar

Usstan xunus naut ssinssrin ulu
Ssinssrin ulu jivviim dos
Ssinssrin ulu jivviim dos
Drill dos cri'n zhah sokoya

Harl l'drathir's orn

Usstan sultha ilta solen

Ilta elamshinae zhah alus

Lu'il zhah tsak xuil ussa a orn

Usstan xunus naut ssinssrin ulu

Ssinssrin ulu jivviim dos

Ssinssrin ulu jivviim dos

Drill dos cri'n zhah sokoya

Usstan xunus naut ssinssrin ulu

Ssinssrin ulu vith xuil dos

Ssinssrin ulu vith xuil dos

Drill dos usst zhah sokoya

Usstan xunus naut ssinssrin tlu

Ssinssrin tlu dossta lince'sa

Ssinssrin tlu dossta lince'sa

Drill Usstan tlun sokoya

Dos jivviim ussa
Usstan jivviim dos
Lu'oh shlu'ta dos xun nindol?
Ka dos zhaunau ussta ssinssrigg

Dos orn'la z'haan tarthe
Drill Usstan belbau rath
Ol morfethen dos ssinssrin mzild
Usstan xunus naut ssinssrin ulu."

Nikodemos found the song beautiful, but from the few words he understood, he knew it was both about death and companionship from the twisted, chaotic dark elf point of view.

He was upset that she cut his hair and shaved his long beard, but he just smiled at her and her beautiful, otherworldly singing. It made him uncontrollably smile. Vhaidra smiled back. Nikodemos noticed that she looked different and mentioned it to her.

She responded with her underworld accent, "While you were sleeping this last week, I ventured around town. For the most part, these humans do not like me. But I found that a half-elf that works at a local bar uses these things. She taught me how to make a stick of beeswax mixed with *pomegranate* and *hyacinth*, that when rubbed on my lips, makes them match the enchanted jacinth gemstones in my armour and daggers. She also taught me how to accent my chartreuse eyes, by rubbing *coal ash* from my eyelids to my eyebrows. She says that it increases your charisma in the overworld."

"I have so many questions! Has it been a week? That is jacinth? I thought jacinth was reddish-orange?"

"Only poor-quality jacinth from the overworld is such a hue. High-quality, pure jacinth from the underworld is a pinkish-purple or magenta colour."

"So, if I remember the usage of enchanted jacinth correctly, you have protection from fire, and your poison daggers cause fire damage too?"

"Not exactly," she smirked, "The enchanted jacinth in my weapons and gloves give burns to those hit by them, but it does not create actual fire. I know elves can see the pinkish-purple magickal flame, but it is not true fire. The jacinth in my boots, circlet, earrings, and choker increase my strength far beyond that of a normal Drow monk, and the gemstones in my armour prevent fire damage.

"Amazing! Anyway, you look very nice, but, of course, you don't need that stick on your lips or that ash on your eyelids to look beautiful."

Vhaidra didn't think it possible, but she blushed, "Being a monk all of this time, I didn't worry about such things of beauty. I only focused on my now-abandoned faith and how to kill with my body, a bone staff, and of course, my throwing daggers."

"Well, the shadow above your eyes does make you look more menacing. So, you still have the look of a killer," he grinned, trying to gain her approval.

She liked that it made her look menacing to the much larger humans. "How do your legs and arms feel?" she asked, changing the subject.

"Tired... for some reason. I'm not sure how that happened since I guess I've just been laying here in this bed for a week. I feel like I have run a marathon!"

"You have been resting for over a week, but I have been exercising them fiercely for you so that you won't lose strength. I am going to keep you on a daily exercise plan to make your body stronger."

"Thanks, now to make sure I don't lose strength, I need to eat. I haven't eaten in a week, I'm famished!"

"Lucky for you, I have food here. Obviously, I have been giving you sips of tea and both the elven healing potions and the medicine from the apothecary, but I could not give you solid food until now."

She presented him a plate of cooked black mushrooms, golden beetroots, red radishes, purple carrots, blue potatoes and white turnips seasoned with turmeric, fenugreek, gold cardamom, holy basil, ginger, green onions, red ginseng, black pepper, smoked sea salt and silverskin garlic.

"Very colourful, Vhaidra!" he excitedly replied, spooning the food into his mouth quickly.

"I may wear all black and have grey skin, but I like my food to be colourful to the eyes and the palate. Different colour foods have different salubrious properties."

"Did you learn cooking in the monastery?"

"Yes, as you may see from the selections, we monks mostly took root vegetables from underneath overworld farms and cooked them with the wild mushrooms growing in the underworld, spiced up by whatever spices could be obtained from the drow spice merchants who travel all over the world."

"Drow spice merchants always have the best spices," he admitted, having, in the past, purchased from the rare drow spice merchant who had come to the overworld to trade or steal exotic spices from all around the world.

"Whether by earning or burning, they definitely do."

Ignoring the comment of how drow spice merchants often illegally got their spices, he took another bite and said, "This is really good, Vhaidra. You are a master chef!"

"Thank you. I was afraid you wouldn't like such food. I hear overworlders like you humans like to eat fatty animal meat, eggs, milk from other beasts, and dry grain-based foods for the most part."

"Oh, we love our meat, but I abstain from meat occasionally as part of my faith, so I eat less meat than many other humans."

"Really, how do you stay so fat then?" she wondered aloud, punching him in his gut and leaving marks from the small teeth in her gloves.

"*Ufgh*! I may abstain from meat and animal products during my fasting periods, but I still love to eat. I am what I eat, and I eat lots of food!" he laughed.

"Not this week, you don't!" she smirked.

Once he had finished, she helped him to the garderobe, and then, helped him walk around to strengthen his legs. They continued this after every meal every day until he was ready to continue their adventure again. By the time he had recovered, he had lost ten kilograms. Vhaidra told Nikodemos that he looked so much better with his short, spiky hair, being clean-shaven and with less weight on his belly.

Nikodemos wasn't sure, but he was glad that she liked it. So, he did not verbally object.

DAY 77

One day, after Vhaidra's physical therapy session for him was completed, Nikodemos asked about this half-elf who Vhaidra mentioned that she had befriended.

"*Ti'erra* has a greathammer and plants it upside down on the floor at the bar named *Brother*. She swings around on it, stripping off her clothes, and the humans drop silver pieces into her stockings and brasserie in exchange."

"Oh, I would never go to such a vile place," Nikodemos remarked.

"Why?" she honestly wondered, "What male would not enjoy such a thing?"

"Besides the fact that it is run by an evil cult of thieves and slavers, it presents women just as a piece of meat. Women are a beautiful flower created by The Ancient of Days, and each flower is intended for only one man, whom the Creator-Logos-Ghost has created for this purpose. Men should only seek out that one flower that he can see in all its glory and only after they are married."

"That is unusual, and I guess a romantic way of looking at it, Hypo, but she needs to make money, and these men are willing to pay. So, who is harmed?"

"Their immortal souls," he sternly answered.

"Hypo, I believe they have free will to do with their souls and bodies whatever they wish."

"I agree. They are free to choose anything, but not all choices are expedient nor spiritually fruitful."

"Perhaps," she conceded. This male was truly different from any male she had ever met before. He was not a slave to his desires, but rather, a slave to his God.

DAY 88

When the day came that they were ready to seek the red dragon again, they followed the same ritual as before, attending the Kyriaki Liturgy and then, an agape feast before they headed for the dungeons at Corinth. *Episkopos Chrysostom* was surprised to see his hypodiakonos with short hair and a clean-shaved face.

"I thought you loved your beard and hair that you were preparing for your ordination to a full *diakonos*, Nikodemos," he asked.

"I did, but mayhap I will learn to love something else more," he blushed.

On the way, Nikodemos finally raised the courage to ask Vhaidra about how she came to be where she was when he found her. Hypo hoped that the time would've made it less painful for her to speak of these events.

"Well, Hypo, as you know, I was a monk. My house came under attack by one of many other houses, and so, I told my archimandrite that I must leave the monastery and defend my house. She forbade me, and so, I killed her, which caused the other monks to descend upon me. I had to kill all of them too."

"What? You killed all the monks in your monastery?"

"Yes, I had to. I took on a lot of damage and unfortunately, lost my beloved, bejewelled bone staff in the process," she continued, "Anyway, by the time I reached my house, there were only a few of my house left, and death was imminent for all members of our house. So, I helped them escape to the overworld. Unfortunately, we immediately ran into seven high elves who drew their weapons and began to attack us."

"How many of your dark elves were there?"

"There were only seven of us as well, including children."

"So, even in my weakened state, I led the battle and took the brunt of their attacks until I could do nothing more. Four of the high elves had died before I noticed that all the members of my house had abandoned me to die at the hands of the three remaining high elves."

"Creator-Logos-Ghost, have mercy!"

"I will allow no mercy on them!" she snarled, "I had fallen, unable to move anymore, and the high elves were about to kill me. Then, you arrived, my saviour," Vhaidra added with a toothy grin.

"The Ancient of Days is the one who directed my steps that day, so truly, He is your Saviour. I am just His instrument."

Rolling her eyes, she added, "Whatever you say, Hypo."

"Vhaidra, I was wondering, did you always have a bad relationship with your archimandrite?"

"Yes. Ever since I moved to *Xunquarra Skete*, I was hated. *Archimandrite Ilphe* hated me. She hated my house, she hated the monastery I had come from, and she hated that I was, in fact, superior to her in every way. She was the cause of me completely losing my faith. I knew that one day, I would have to kill her."

"Where were you before?"

"I was in *Yochlol Lavra* before. I was there from my youth. My archimandrite there, *Halisstra*, adored me and taught me all the hidden, secret, and ancient fighting styles of the Drow monks. She called me *'The Chosen One,'* and even gave me daily *bright light training*."

"Wow! Why did you leave there?" Nikodemos inquired, "And what is 'bright light training?'"

"Well, she told me that she had taught me all that she could and that I had to move on to Archimandrite Ilphe's Monastery to learn my final lesson. I'm sure she was right, as Halisstra was wise beyond her lengthy one thousand years, but I am not sure what I was supposed to learn at Xunquarra Skete. As for bright light training, she taught me to fight in the bright light, something I continued at the Skete. My vision is not even half as good as you overworlders in the sunlight, but my eyes have been trained to see well enough to fight."

"So, do you know what my face looks like?"

"Yes, Hypo, I have it committed to memory, now that you no longer look like a lycanthrope, and all that beastly hair is off of it!" she smiled.

Nikodemos smiled back and added, "Maybe, you already learned what she wanted you to learn, and are not aware, or maybe, she knew the political situation, and you would have to flee and would learn it here above?"

"Maybe."

"Or maybe, she knew you would kill all the members of Xunquarra Skete, the very same monastery that hated her Yochlol Lavra?"

"Could be. I just think it was supposed to be something deeper."

"Maybe, we'll figure it out together."

"I'd like that. Well, we are at the entrance now. Let's descend."

"Indeed."

This time, the dungeon was oddly cleared of all monsters on their journey, so they made it to the lair of the red dragon without any distractions, save for a burned *cyclops* body contorted with multiple broken bones in the hallway. The cyclops had the design of a fist carved into his chest. Nikodemos said another prayer right before they entered the last room, the large circular room of the red dragon!

CHAPTER III
DRAGON HUNT

"A dead cyclops; this is an ominous sign." Nikodemos whispered.

Vhaidra agreed and wondered why it had something carved into its chest, but that concern would have to wait. She feared fighting the dragon on the ground, as her daggers would be useless against the strong but light dragon scales. Her only hope was that the young dragon would fly into the air. She grabbed Nikodemos' arm hard and confided this fear to him. He told her not to worry as they entered the final chamber of the dungeon. Vhaidra still worried. She wished she still had her unbreakable bone staff.

When they entered and saw the small male dragon, Nikodemos called for Vhaidra to get behind him, but she had already scurried to the shadows of this round treasure room, preparing her throwing daggers to pierce the soft underbelly of this dragon, should it be available for attack. Vhaidra trusted Hypo and had fire protection from the mystical jacinth gemstones in her armour, but she was not about to be purposely in the eye of a fire attack.

The hypodiakonos muttered under his breath, "I hope this works!"

Nikodemos next called out to the dragon and threw Qing Long at full strength, just missing the head of the red beast, where it implanted itself into the ceiling of the dungeon chamber. The red dragon flew up into the air, looked closely at Qing Long's motif and appraised its value, mentally adding it to the value of his belongings. The dragon then laughed, preparing his fire breath attack.

Nikodemos threw holy water in a cruciform manner at the beast, only angering it, and then, he started reciting the following chant, "For the rest, my brethren, and keep on being empowered in the Creator-Logos-Ghost and in the strength of His might. Put on the full *Armour of The Ancient of Days*, for you to be able to stand against the wiles of the devils..."

Vhaidra had no idea what Hypo was doing. Was he trying to commit suicide? There were better ways to do such a thing! But she couldn't be worried about his intent now; his life was solely in his God's hands now.

As Nikodemos continued chanting, Vhaidra threw her first volley of poison daggers and scurried to another place. As she expected, this caught the attention of the dragon, and he spit fire at the spot where Vhaidra formerly had been. She continued this tactic twelve more times and then, the dragon shot fire where she was going to go next. She stopped and reconsidered her plan of attack. The small dragon stopped looking for her, feeling sick from all the poisoned daggers. Instead, the dragon now decided to shoot a blast of fire directly at Nikodemos. The crimson wyrm had turned around a full three hundred and sixty degrees, trying to get Vhaidra.

Nikodemos was still continuing his chanting, holding his holy symbol around his neck out to the dragon, "...For this cause take up the full Armour of The Ancient of Days, in order that ye might be able to withstand in the evil day, and having counteracted all things, to stand. Stand therefore, having girded your loins with Truth, and having put on for yourselves the *Breastplate of Righteousness*, and having shod your feet in *Boots of Preparedness*; on the whole, take up the *Shield of Faith,* with which ye shall be able to quench all the fiery darts of the evil one..." as the fire came down upon him.

Vhaidra could not dare to look as the fire hit its intended target. She screamed and threw another volley of poisoned daggers. Instead of the flames engulfing Hypo, it danced around him!

Vhaidra, who somehow instinctively knew that Hypo was going to be alright, continued her attack, but now, she was moving in the opposite direction and changing the distance between her attacks, in case the dragon learned her pattern and predicted where to aim his fiery attack.

The red dragon was becoming weaker from the sheer number of poisoned daggers in its underbelly. He lowered his altitude and dropped his tail and back feet to the ground. Hypo continued his chant as he began running up the poisoned dragon's tail, and continued up to its back and up to its neck.

Once he got to the beginning of the spine of the dragon, he finished with, "...And take the *Helmet of Salvation*, and the *Sword of The Spirit*, which is the

Logos of The Ancient of Days – by means of every prayer and entreaty, praying in every season in the *Spirit,* and being vigilant towards this same thing with all perseverance and entreaty for all the saints, and for me... *Amin.*"

He then leapt in the air, glowing with the armour of *Uncreated Light,* and pulled the Qing Long from out the ceiling. Grasping the bottom of the handle of his weapon and swinging it, it seemingly transformed into a *greatsword* made out of the same light, and unbelievably, sliced the poisoned dragon's head off in three fell swoops.

Vhaidra stood astonished as she watched the rest of the dragon come crashing down. Hypo awkwardly crashed down on top of its severed head, and the summoned armour disappeared.

She asked, "By the Dark Mother, how did you do that?"

He smiled, and said, "By The Ancient of Days' *providence,* and because you distracted and weakened it with all those poison daggers. Thank you!"

Vhaidra wasn't sure how much credit she could claim. The cleric had done some powerful works in here tonight. She punched him in the arm, inadvertently making him bleed, due to what he had assumed were small horns on the knuckles.

She instructed him, "Don't ever make me worry like that ever again!"

While Hypo gathered the dragon's stolen treasures, a still-astonished Vhaidra started to skin the giant flying lizard.

"Why are you doing that?" Nikodemos asked.

Vhaidra replied, "I am going to make you some red dragon scale armour. It is lighter, stronger, and gives you more coverage than that primitive chainmail armour you wear under your robes. As you now know, chainmail won't stop sylvan arrows or my tooth-covered knuckles!"

It was now Nikodemos' turn to be astonished. He had never heard of using dragon skin as scale armour. "Those are teeth on your knuckles? I thought they were horns! You never fail to amaze me, Vhaidra."

She smiled at him, and retorted, "This is nothing; slaying a dragon in one slice is truly amazing!"

"It was three slices, but you can thank The Ancient of Days for that, Vhaidra," he said, kissing his icon.

Thinking over the battle, she added, "That was a long chant. I guess you were right; it is good that I was able to distract the dragon while you chanted."

"I was depending on that," he smirked.

Once they were all packed up, they left the deserted dungeon with packs full of treasure and dragon skin. Nikodemos carried the small dragon's head. Once they left, they took the head and gave it, along with ten per cent of the treasure, to Corinth's episkopos. The episkopos, *Grigorios,* blessed them and gave the cleric a powerful relic, the *Timiou Stavrou* on a rope chain. Nikodemos kissed it, put it around his neck, gave his old silver neck chain with the Symbol of The Way to Episkopos Grigorios and kissed his hand. Then, they left, taking his blessing.

That night, they stayed at an inn to sleep in Corinth before they returned by hired cart to their city of residence, Sicyon. Unfortunately for them, it would not be the restful night that they had hoped for...

CHAPTER IV
EYE TO DIE

The adventurers cleaned and sharpened their weapons before going to sleep. Just as the pair settled into their beds at the inn, there were the sounds of screaming. Then, shaking of the earth. Next, the destruction of the outer wall of the inn.

A low, gravelly voice rang out, "You kill Grok's brother, and Grok kills you!"

Vhaidra grabbed her armour and daggers while Nikodemos just grabbed his robes and his Yan Yue Dao. There was no time for him to put on complicated chain armour.

From the second floor, they could clearly see who had attacked the inn. It was a giant cyclops!

"Who killed Grok's brother? Who killed Grok's brother's master?"

"I think he means us, Vhaidra!" Nikodemos shouted.

"But we didn't kill that cyclops!" Vhaidra replied.

"I'm not sure we can convince him of that!" he replied. Jumping from the second floor, he pierced the foot of the giant, slicing one of his tendons on the top of his foot.

Vhaidra yelled at the cyclops in the common language of the underworld, telling him that they killed the red dragon, but not the cyclops. Unfortunately, the one-eyed monster, Grok, did not believe her.

Grok painfully screamed, "You kill Grok's brother, Gorn. Grok kills you!"

Vhaidra threw a volley of poisoned daggers while Nikodemos pulled Qing Long out of the top of the giant's foot and ran towards his Achilles tendon on the other foot.

Vhaidra kept talking to the Cyclops, trying to get him to stop, "We did kill the red dragon, Grok, but Gorn was already dead when we got there!" Vhaidra added, "Gorn's master killed Gorn, so we killed Gorn's Master!"

"No, you kill Gorn! Grok kill you!" the beast replied, then screamed in pain as his Achilles tendon was sliced in half, causing him to fall backwards to the ground, the back of his head hitting a large, sharp rock.

Nikodemos ran back up to the second floor and checked on Vhaidra. When he saw that she was fine, he ran to the now-missing wall and then, leapt as high and as far into the air as he could, holding his weapon behind him.

"What is that crazy human doing now?" Vhaidra asked, shaking her head with her mouth agape.

Nikodemos flipped his Yan Yue Dao around and landed with the blade in the eye of the Cyclops. It went all the way through the eye, into the brain, and then stuck into the skull. The velocity of the landing, along with the sudden stop, broke the weapon clean in half and flung the cleric over the head of Grok into a pile of dung.

Nikodemos looked at his broken weapon handle and painfully cried out, "Qing Long!"

The cyclops was writhing in pain, screaming and unable to get up. Besides the damage to his feet and the base of his skull, the human's weapon had broken off in his eye and brain, doing acid damage. Grok grabbed for the weapon, to pull it out, but no part of the weapon stuck out for the one-eyed monster to pull it out.

Vhaidra ran out to Nikodemos and looked at the broken handle of Qing Long. It had broken into a very sharp point. Vhaidra kicked him to make him relax his grip and pulled it out of his hand. She then ran over to the prone cyclops and thrust the sharp broken handle completely into the heart of the giant, doing more acid damage. Grok's hand grabbed for her, so she jumped in the air and threw poison daggers into the beast's jugular veins. Grok continued to cry out in pain, hitting the ground for a few more minutes, until he finally stopped moving. Then, as usual, Vhaidra collected her daggers from the corpse of the beast.

Nikodemos was still crying about his lost weapon. Vhaidra comforted him and told him that she was sure that he would obtain another *great weapon* soon. With the treasure they collected from the gelatinous cube, wood and high elves, red dragon and now, the cyclops, they could get him almost any weapon in the world. Finally, he calmed down. They travelled to another inn. However, Nikodemos insisted on paying the first innkeeper for the damages to the inn, even though it was not their fault.

"The cyclops attacked the inn, seeking us, Vhaidra; it is the right thing to do," he explained.

Vhaidra just shook her head in disbelief. Seeing that Hypo's robes were ruined, she stayed up all night working on the red dragon scale armour she was making for him.

Nikodemos bathed and sobbed over the loss of his beloved Qing Long while chanting and drinking healing potions to help him heal from Vhaidra's kick and earlier punch to his shoulder.

CHAPTER V
LESSER AND GREATER

DAY 89

In the morning, the duo headed back to Sicyon. Nikodemos wore the new dragon scale armour which Vhaidra had fashioned. He loved it. It was actually very comfortable and weighed much less than his chainmail. So, they sold the old armour.

While his cloth boots looked funny with the scale armour, he did not find any other footgear, nor any weapons that he wanted to buy.

When they arrived in the city, Nikodemos put on a fresh white robe and a black vest over the dragon scale armour, and sought out his Episkopos, to whom he also wanted to give ten per cent of their treasure. Vhaidra figured he could do whatever he wanted with up to fifty per cent of the treasure, so she did not object or hit him.

When they found the episkopos, he was in an excited mood. "The *Elder* told me that you were able to successfully call upon The Ancient of Days' Armour when you fought the red dragon that was harassing Corinth!"

He replied to the episkopos, "Yes, it is true. I followed the example of Presbyteros Romanos in Zhong."

"Well, then, it is time for you to take it up full-time," the episkopos remarked and led them to a catacomb hermitage. Nikodemos was confused as to what the episkopos had meant by this but obediently followed, with Vhaidra to his side. In a cell of the catacomb, a *hermitage,* was the whole Armour of The Ancient of Days, glowing brightly with the elder kneeling nearby, reading prayers from a holy book. *Episkopos Chrysostom* announced their arrival as soon as the prayer ended. "*Elder Dionysios,* Hypodiakonos Nikodemos is here."

The elder wore the *great schema* over his heavy greying black wool robes at all times. It was greyish black, decorated with many powerful religious symbols of The Way (including angels, spears, skulls, among others), which were made of white cloth. The great schema was a symbol of his enlightenment and detachment from the world. Because of the oversized hood, his face remained hidden. One could only see his long greyish-brown beard (dreadlocked from years of not being combed or washed) and his weathered greenish-grey sandaled feet with long uncut yellowed toenails. He kept his hands together in front of him so that they, along with his chotki (a prayer rope), were always hidden in the large flowing sleeves of his robe. He preferred to stay away from the world in his catacomb hermitage, but the Armour had other plans for him.

"Shouldn't he be an *ierodiakonos* if he is to wear the Armour?" the elder asked Episkopos Chrysostom.

"No, Elder Dionysios, Hypodiakonos Nikodemos refuses to become a diakonos until he marries, as he does not wish to become a monk."

"Very well. Hypodiakonos Nikodemos, you are the one who called on the Armour and defeated the red dragon?"

"Yes, Elder," Nikodemos replied.

"And this was the first time you have ever done this?"

"Yes, Elder. I learned it from Presbyteros Romanos when I was in the land of Zhong."

"Then, it is yours now. Put it on over your chainmail," Elder Dionysios instructed.

"Elder, I no longer have my chainmail; I sold it after my companion, Vhaidra, made me new armour out of the red dragon's skin."

"Your companion? Is she to be your wife?" the elder bluntly asked.

"She is not of our faith, Elder Dionysios," he replied quickly, seemingly avoiding the question.

Vhaidra noted the conversation and decided that she would ask what this all meant at a more appropriate time. With all this theological talk, she figured she would excuse herself as soon as it seemed an acceptable time.

"Very well, put it on over your scale armour then," instructed the elder.

"What is the armour made of?" Vhaidra asked, "It looks like it is made of glass with lightning inside!"

"It looks like polished gold armour, reflecting a bright sun, to me," added Nikodemos.

"It is made of the *Uncreated Light,*" the elder explained.

"Solid light? Wow!" Vhaidra replied. She had never heard of any such thing. This truly was a *powerful relic.*

Hypodiakonos Nikodemos put on the *Boots of Preparation*, the *Girdle of Truth*, the *Breastplate of Righteousness*, the *Cloak of Zeal*, the *Helmet of Salvation*, and the *Gauntlets of Vengeance*. Then, he strapped onto his arm the *Shield of Faith* and picked up the two-handed *Greatsword of the Spirit* that was as big as his beloved Yan Yue Dao had been.

Each piece, save for the girdle, had the faint design of a double-headed eagle. The symbol filled the shield, it was the design of the hilt of the sword, it wrapped around the arms on the gauntlets, it took up most of the breastplate, it wrapped around the legs on the boots, and it was on the cowl-less cloak as well. The helmet actually had the symbol on the left and right side. The girdle had a simple cruciform design that took up the whole garment. There were additional cruciform designs on the pieces covering the knees, feet and the back of the hands.

The red of the dragon scales and the golden glow of the Uncreated Light looked amazing together, Vhaidra thought. This surely must be his destiny.

"Now, you must know that I am the keeper of the Armour of The Ancient of Days, so I will now forever be your cell attendant. Where the armour goes, I also go," the elder exclaimed.

"I am honoured," Nikodemos replied. "I will need someone to teach me how to use a greatsword and shield properly, anyway, as I have regularly only used a Yan Yue Dao, a great weapon, before."

"Yes, this is my duty as well, Nikodemos."

"Thank you, Elder Dionysios!"

Vhaidra excused herself and departed the episkopos, the elder, and the hypodiakonos, and visited her friend, Ti'erra.

Ti'erra had bad news. She wanted to move on, but the men that owned the bar had enslaved all the working girls and no longer let them keep their earnings or leave of their own volition. This confirmed what Hypo had said, that it was a gang and a cult. There were too many people in this town of Sicyon that were part of it. So, she was afraid that she could never escape. Vhaidra promised her that she and Hypo would help. Ti'erra suggested that in an hour, it could be a good time to stage an escape.

She went to Nikodemos' home and told Elder Dionysios and Hypo, who had just arrived there, about this.

"Hypo, she is my friend. We must save her. This is *justice* to you, no?"

"You are right. But if we rescue her, we will need to abandon Sicyon and hideaway. The gang and cult that owns *Brother* are too numerous for us to fight off ourselves."

"Is that sacrifice too much?" she asked.

"The price of one soul; it is beyond measure. We must save her, body and soul," he replied.

"The Armour calls us to action much too soon," mumbled Elder Dionysios, who was kneeling nearby. The three packed up their belongings that they would need, and then, they all went to the club at the pre-appointed time.

Ti'erra was a very young at eighty-two years of age and had medium golden-brown skin, elvish ears, curly reddish-brown bunned and braided hair that was butt-length, and as she liked to point out, she was very well-rounded everywhere. The dwelf wore a green suede smock dress with light golden-brown edging. Her boots and gloves were golden-brown with green edging. She held a six-foot-long greathammer encrusted with aquamarine gemstones, which gave it a freezing attack. The only enchantment that she knew was charming others, although she had a very strong sense of intuition. It helped her make money when doing her hammer dances. She was only four feet and five inches tall, so her weapon was much taller than her.

The group was met near the door by Ti'erra. "Hi, Monk, I just got done dancing, and the gang are in a meeting now. So, now is the perfect time to escape."

Nikodemos looked down at the female who was much shorter than Vhaidra and asked, "I thought you were a half-elf?"

"I am. I am half sylvan and half-dwarf," Ti'erra explained.

"Oh, ok, you are a dwelf!"

Ti'erra was actually short enough that she could see the elder's face clearly from where she stood. She gave him a knowing wink.

"And being half-dwarf is why I have a larger head, larger breasts, larger belly, larger butt, larger feet, and larger muscles than her too!" she laughed as she changed her gaze to Vhaidra and then to the hypodiakonos. "I like your polished light *topaz* armour, Cleric!"

"Thank you, but it is actually Uncreated Light armour," Nikodemos replied.

Elder Dionysios mumbled, "It is the armour of our God!"

"The cleric is a God?" Ti'erra asked and bowed down in prostration before him.

"By the Dark Mother, no! He is not a God; it is the Armour of their God, The Ancient of Days!" Vhaidra hissed, grabbing her by the arm roughly and picking her up, "Let's get out of here, and we can discuss this more later before we get killed trying to save you!"

The solitary human bouncer stepped up to stop their exit, but Vhaidra quickly defeated him by hitting him with hard, precise attacks on his temples, larynx, the base of his nose, and the tip of his breastbone with her fingers. The quick, silent attack was not noticed by any of the drunken patrons, but the bartender noticed and ran into the attached conference room to alert the gang of the events taking place.

The four exited the bar and clubhouse and headed down the alley. When they were almost out of the alley, a group of six muscular men with studded leather armour, carrying maces and morning stars, yelled from the club's exit, telling them to come back now. The dwelf and her rescuers started to run, and Elder Dionysios, the slowest of the four, started reciting a chant.

Suddenly, four powerful warhorses with long flowing manes and tails appeared in front of them; one white with moonstone armour, one black with *jet* armour, one red with *topaz* armour, and one pale yellow with *jade* armour. The elder jumped on the white horse and told the others to choose horses as well. Vhaidra chose the black horse, Nikodemos grabbed the short dwelf, Ti'erra, placing her on the yellow horse and took the red horse for himself. The four raced out of Sicyon faster than imaginable as the Elder continued to chant, causing black storm clouds to cover the city. An immense storm brewed, and lightning struck their six pursuers dead as well as striking the *Brother* bar.

The elder cried out, "To the *Valley of the Tombs*!"

"After you, Mighty *Wizard*!" Ti'erra giggled, and all four raced atop their horses to the southeast.

CHAPTER VI
UNTO DEATH

The horses were as quick as lightning, and the four passengers rode close together on the long ride.

"So, tell me about yourself, Ti'erra. I'd like to get to know the lady we've risked our hide and homes for," Nikodemos queried.

"Should I start at the beginning?" Ti'erra asked.

"No better place," Nikodemos replied with a smile.

"Well, I was conceived after a great battle where gold dwarves and sylvan came together to fight a mutual enemy which cannot be spoken of. There was much celebrating, and my mother, a gold dwarf, consummated her night of drinking with one or more sylvan. My mother raised me as a dwarf, but I never really fit in, because I was taller than everyone else and..."

"Well that explains things," Hypo interjected.

"What do you mean, Cleric?" Ti'erra asked.

"You never had a father and had a troubled childhood."

"Right."

"No wonder you ended up dancing nude for random men."

"Hypo!" Vhaidra screamed as she hit him across the face with one of her ponytail whips.

"Nikodemos, do not judge," Elder Dionysios mumbled.

Nikodemos held his face in pain and explained, "Ow! I didn't mean to judge. I was just trying to logically see what would cause you to descend... err... take up such a profession."

"No problem. You are probably right," Ti'erra conceded with a smile. "How about you, Monk? What's your story?"

"I really don't like to talk about my life in the underworld, but upon my arrival in the overworld, I was almost killed until Hypo saved me. I have been with him ever since."

Nikodemos then realised that he should be honoured to know her underworld past if she really did not like speaking of it to others.

"Who is *Hypo*?" asked the elder.

"Ugh, Nikodemos introduced himself as Hypo... Diak... onos... Niko... Demos in a broken underworld language, and so, I called him Hypo. He's been Hypo to me ever since."

"That's sweet," Ti'erra swooned.

Vhaidra just growled and rolled her eyes.

"How about you, Wizard?" Ti'erra asked.

"My conception was not as happy an event as yours, Ti'erra. My father raped my mother."

"Oh my!" she replied.

"My mother put me in an orphanage, unable to take care of a freak like me. So, the female monks of *Transfiguration Cenobium* raised me until I became a monastic myself. Over time, The Ancient of Days blessed me to become an elder and the Guardian of His Armour."

"You are a *monk*?" Vhaidra asked.

Elder Dionysios explained, "I am not a fighting monk like you, Vhaidra. I am an ascetic monk who learned how to call upon the Power of the Will of The Ancient of Days by chanting. I have no martial abilities at all, outside of my brute strength I inherited from my worldly father."

"I understand how hard it is to not fit into the culture you are raised in, Wizard."

Nikodemos added, "It was different for him than you, Ti'erra. He was an orphan, but not an outcast because of his looks or race."

"You are wrong, Nikodemos," the elder explained.

Ti'erra explained, "You've never seen his face before, have you, Cleric?"

"No. Why? Why am I wrong?"

"He's a half-orc," Ti'erra explained.

Nikodemos was shocked. He felt stupid. It explained the elder's foot colour and why he made sure to keep his hands and face hidden at all times. "I never knew, Elder Dionysios. Sorry."

"It is ok. I have kept this hidden from most. It is why I live in a hermitage in the catacombs and not in a cenobitic monastery."

"He's beautiful and strong," Ti'erra sang, "What's your story, Cleric?"

"Nothing interesting. Just a human, raised by his human father and a human mother. I have been in the service of the Temple as an acolyte, a kantoros, an anagnostis, and now, as a hypodiakonos. On my birthday, the one hundred sixty-sixth day of the year, The Ancient of Days directed me as I was doing my chotki prayers, and I came upon three large male high elves attacking a beautiful female dark elf who could not move. I recognised those high elves as being the same ones who desecrated our temple earlier this year."

Vhaidra blushed and finally realised why he had called those three high elves *heretics.*

"I yelled at them to stop, and they ignored me. So, I stood between those damned high elves and the dark elf, Vhaidra, and used my trusty Yan Yue Dao to beat them down into surrender. Then, I nursed Vhaidra back to health. Ever since, we've been inseparable partners connected at the hip."

Ti'erra giggled, "How romantic!" and Vhaidra grew even flusher, neither one realising the innocent meaning of his slang term. To an elf, it sounded like he was saying that they were to be mates.

"Vhaidra returned the favour, saving me from sure death from three wood elf ranger-assassins. In nursing me back to health, she cut my hair short and shaved off my beard. She also made me a dragon scale armour out of the corpse of a red dragon that we had defeated together. Recently, I was graced with the Armour of The Ancient of Days, and its trusted Guardian, Elder Dionysios."

"So, you used to have a dwarven style beard with long hair, not unlike the wizard?" Ti'erra inquired.

"Exactly!" Vhaidra explained, "I wanted to see what he looked like with a proper elven-style haircut and no beard, and that is why he looks so handsome today."

"That and Vhaidra's delicious meals and exercise regimen caused me to lose all my fat."

"Well, most of it anyway," she smirked.

"Why would sylvan attack you, Cleric?"

"It was because of me, Ti'erra," Vhaidra started to explain before she was interrupted.

"Everybody put their legs up!" the elder instructed.

"Huh? Why?" Nikodemos asked.

"Just do as I told you. Put your feet up at the horse's eyes and drop all of your belongings, NOW!"

As the elder finished his words, the four horses faded into the ether. The adventurers' inertia sent them flying forward. The pose that they were in helped them land properly, doing somersaults until they came to a full stop.

"By the Dark Mother, could we have got more warning?" Vhaidra asked with a glare, spitting sand out of her mouth.

"My apologies," murmured Elder Dionysios, "Now that we are now at the Valley of the Tombs, we simply no longer needed those horses."

Nikodemos got up, and Vhaidra gasped. He had a deep vertical gash over the middle of his left eye, from his eyebrow to the top of his cheekbone. She saw his blood from this wound on the end of her ponytail. She realised she had inadvertently done this when using her hair as a whip in anger.

"I'm so sorry, Hypo!" She ran over, comforted her rescuer and began to wash the sand out of the wound.

"Just a flesh wound, it will heal," he replied with a smile.

Elder Dionysios gathered firewood while Ti'erra set up camp and Vhaidra cooked dinner. Nikodemos boiled tea for drinking and prepared to take care of his wounds while he chanted healing prayers.

Everyone changed into sleeping clothes, except for the elder, who always wore the same clothes. Vhaidra offered to wash their clothes for the day. She had made Nikodemos a black short-sleeved shirt and short pants out of specially treated spider silk that matched her black short pants and camisole which she made for sleeping while in Sicyon. Ti'erra wore a green baby-doll nightgown.

The elder explained he only needed two hours of sleep a night so that he would sleep for two hours then take watch. Vhaidra offered to do her four hours of elven reverie after those initial two hours so that neither Nikodemos nor Ti'erra needed to take watch. Ti'erra only needed to sleep six hours a night but enjoyed getting eight hours when she could.

With that decided, they all went to sleep, except for Vhaidra who washed the clothes and then, sat by Hypo, caressing his injured face as he slept. It was an uneventful night, but the same could not be said for the morning.

CHAPTER VII
INTO THE AMISS

DAY 90

When they awoke in the morning, the elder and the Armour of The Ancient of Days were gone.

"Elder Dionysios left during his watch and took the armour, including the sword and shield!" Nikodemos cried out.

"Let's wait before we jump to conclusions, Cleric," replied Ti'erra.

"Armour up!" Vhaidra commanded, "Weapons at ready!"

The three put on their armour, which for Nikodemos, would be only his dragon scale armour with no boots, having abandoned his cloth boots when he had received the Boots of Preparation.

Ti'erra searched the ground. She saw abandoned sandals and orc-like footprints of the wizard, but those footprints only went in circles. There were, however, a lot of little footprints. They headed to and from a cave nearby. She picked up the sandals and gave them to Nikodemos to wear.

"We're going into the cave," she instructed.

"Why?" Nikodemos asked.

"Because that is where we will find your armour and the wizard."

"How do you know?"

"Trust me, Cleric!" said Ti'erra.

Ti'erra instructed the cleric not to light any torches and for Vhaidra to lead him in the darkness. Being a dwelf, she had a very good dark and night vision too.

They headed through a long cavern that curved then narrowed and eventually, led to a high opening over a large room full of *goblins*! There, in the room below, was the Armour of The Ancient of Days, displayed on stakes and the elder, tied-up and his mouth gagged, lying on an *altar*. Without being able to speak, he could not chant to defend himself.

The goblins were worshipping the glowing armour. At their *shaman's* instructions, all their torches had been exhausted. The only light came from a nearby campfire and the Armour itself.

"There are a lot of goblins!" Nikodemos whispered, "What can we do? I have neither a weapon nor a shield!"

Ti'erra had a plan. One of the party's members would need to distract the goblins. Another one of them would need to sneak and unbind the wizard. The cleric would need to grab his sword and start swinging, and then, whoever was with him would take over fighting to give him time to suit up in his Armour.

Vhaidra agreed. She offered to be the distractor, throwing daggers from her high perch. She asked Ti'erra to guide Nikodemos through the dark cavern to get in position to claim his armour. Ti'erra would pull out the gag and cut the binds on the elder.

Once Ti'erra and Nikodemos made it to their positions, Ti'erra called out, "Now, Vhaidra!"

The goblins started to panic as daggers started to appear in the backs of their fellow goblins. In a short time, they regained their composure; they figured out where the daggers were coming from and started throwing spears towards Vhaidra. So, she retreated. The goblin shaman jumped on top of Elder Dionysius with a wicked-looking, enchanted *ruby* dagger.

Ti'erra knocked the goblin shaman down off of the elder. Taking out the gag, she effortlessly loosened the bonds around Elder Dionysios, and he began to chant. Then, Nikodemos grabbed his sword and began to swing it around, knocking back many goblins, including the shaman.

Nikodemos commanded Ti'erra to start throwing the dead goblin bodies into the fire.

"Why, Cleric?"

"Just trust me and do it!"

"Aye, aye, Cleric!"

Ti'erra did as she was instructed, and then, began to hammer down on the surrounding living goblins.

The goblins had now focused on Ti'erra as Nikodemos finished putting his Armour on.

Vhaidra sent another volley of daggers into the backs of the goblins and then, started chanting herself.

At the same time, one by one, the still-burning skeletons in the fire rose up and started to attack the still-living goblins, and a plague of venomous vipers rose from the ground biting the remaining goblins. Nikodemos and Ti'erra continued to attack with their weapons as well. The goblin shaman had frozen arms from Ti'erra's enchanted greathammer attack and so, he retreated, chanting to turn invisible to make his escape.

After a short while, the goblins were all extinguished, save for a few remaining burning goblin skeletons that fought among themselves.

"Thank you!" muttered the elder, as Ti'erra gave him his sandals that the Cleric had discarded after putting on his armoured boots.

Vhaidra gave the dead goblins a boot party, tearing them up with her horned boots.

The team went back up to their base camp, packed up after their breakfast and then, headed back down into the cave as Nikodemos wanted to find the missing goblin shaman. The elder agreed that travelling through the cave, and hence, staying hidden, was a good idea. There they collected treasure, potions, and rations. Nikodemos noticed that there were eight ways to go out of the room, not including the way they had entered.

"Which way should we go?" Nikodemos asked.

"I have a great way to decide!" Ti'erra answered and pulled out a bag of dice. She rolled an eight-sided die and got a four. She counted off the passages, pointed to the fourth one and said, "This way!" She led the group to their next adventure.

The adventurers went through the tight pathway, and once they got to the next room, Vhaidra screamed in pure horror, jumping into Nikodemos' arms.

CHAPTER VIII
CORRODED CAVERN

Nikodemos' armour lit up the room so that everyone could see what had made Vhaidra scream in horror. There, in the middle of the room, was a nest of *rust monsters* feeding on the armour of a dead drow *shadow knight.* The rust monsters looked at the adventurers and then, went back to their meal of metal armour and weapons.

Nikodemos knew of Vhaidra's extreme fear of rust monsters, which is why she wore no metal at all. Now that his necklace had been replaced by the relic of the Timiou Stavrou on a rope chain as well as his chain mail being replaced by the red dragon scale armour, he also wore no metal. He wasn't sure of the others. The elder possibly had a silver Symbol of The Way, but more likely for an elder, who rejected materialism, it would be made of simple hemp rope. Ti'erra's greathammer was leather, stone, and wood, but he did not know if she had metal clasps or jewellery.

He shouted out the command, "Ti'erra, hammer time!" and Ti'erra went into action, smashing and freezing the rust monsters.

Honestly, the rust monsters really were no threat to them, but Nikodemos pretended as if they did, due to Vhaidra's phobia. He whispered to her, "Vhaidra, we need you to animate that skeleton."

She punched him in the face and said, "By the Dark Mother, no!" But she knew he was right. She was shaking in fear but was able to recite her chant, allowing the skeleton of the dead shadow knight to rise and begin to attack the rust monsters. With both of its swords being eaten by the rust monsters, the skeleton used large rocks it picked up in its hands to attack.

"Now, use your acid cloud," Nikodemos whispered in her pointed ear.

She trembled and chanted again, and the armour and weapons that were being feasted on were surrounded in a cloud of chartreuse acid. It slowly weakened the monsters eating the metal as they inhaled the acid cloud.

Elder Dionysios motioned to Nikodemos to hand Vhaidra to him. Nikodemos complied, and the elder chanted. Then, the elder was able to levitate over the room to the elevated exit, where he placed Vhaidra. Nikodemos began to use the Sword of The Spirit, joining Ti'erra in the attack against the creatures.

Thankfully, Nikodemos figured out that Ti'erra wore only suede leather and her greathammer was made out of wood and stone, braced together with leather. Her earrings were actually bone earrings, a gift from Vhaidra. The elder also wore no metal, having only his heavy wool robes, his great schema, his hemp necklace and leather sandals.

In time, the monsters were all destroyed, and Nikodemos went to check on Vhaidra, who just held him tight. "Thank you, Hypo. Thank you!"

"You're welcome, Vhaidra; anything for you."

She looked in his eyes, seeing that the damage she had done with her ponytail whips had actually hurt his left eye, and she also saw that his words were true from his heart, and so, she kissed him, not any longer being bothered by his beard that was growing back. He kissed her back.

"This may not be the last dark elf we encounter," the elder mentioned.

"We are not in the underworld yet, but it is possible we may see some," Vhaidra explained.

"Do you have the symbol of your house, should we encounter any?"

"No, it was destroyed in my battle to get out of my monastery."

"May I recommend we take the jet symbol of the house from that skeleton? In the future, it may be good for you to pretend that you are a *slaver* with us as slaves, should we encounter any more dark elves."

"Agreed, Elder. If we encounter any drow, all of you hold your hands together, look at your feet and respond to any questions with, 'Yes, *Mistress.*'"

"Yes, Mistress!" Ti'erra quipped.

Vhaidra just rolled her eyes, and then smiled, not admitting that she liked the sound of it.

The earth under Ti'erra started to shake, and then, she launched into the air as a huge *bulette* appeared from the earth in which she had stood. The bulette sniffed towards Ti'erra and was disinterested. It also sniffed towards Vhaidra and was equally disinterested, not liking the taste of dwarves or elves.

The bulette instead launched itself towards Nikodemos. Vhaidra jumped down from the elevated exit. She flung her poisoned, throwing daggers into the underside of the beast. It screamed in pain and took a bite of Nikodemos' leg. It was unable to bite through the Boots of Preparation, so it flung him across the room towards their initial entrance.

The bulette now eyed Dionysios, who had no armour and no weapons. As it began to leap at its prey, Ti'erra used her greathammer to smash and freeze the creature's tail, pinning it to the ground. It was unable to leap forward. The creature screamed in pain again and did its best to turn around. Ti'erra, now having distracted the bulette, lifted her hammer and struck the creature again, before it could leap at her. She hit it in the back, smashing it down against the ground and shoving the poisoned daggers, now lodged in its belly, deeper into its organs. When it screamed in pain again, Vhaidra threw three more daggers into its mouth.

Nikodemos returned to the scene of the battle now and followed up Vhaidra's attack by shoving his greatsword down the throat of the monster. He then picked up the beast and flipped it over his head, exposing its underside, which Vhaidra and Ti'erra attacked with a volley of daggers followed by a hammer attack, driving them deep into the beast's organs. Nikodemos twisted his sword as he pulled it out of the dying animal's body.

"Wizard, you need armour!" Ti'erra cried out.

"The Great Schema is all the armour I will ever wear," Dionysios explained.

"Then, you need a weapon of some sort!" Ti'erra explained.

"Elders do not use weapons; only chants."

"You need something to fend off attacks."

Ti'erra whispered something to the cleric, causing Vhaidra to give her a nasty look, and then, the hypodiakonos said, "Elder Dionysios, will a walking staff be acceptable? Walking in these dungeons can be precarious!"

"Ok," he conceded in a low mumble.

"Yay!" shouted Ti'erra, "Now, let's eat dinner!"

Nikodemos pushed the bodies of the rust monsters into the hole that the bulette had come out of, trying to keep them out of sight of Vhaidra. He was not sure if her irrational fear extended to dead rust monsters too.

The group built a fire and prepared their rations for their midday meal. Vhaidra apologised again for hurting Nikodemos' eye and punching him in the face, while she dug her daggers out of the dead bulette. He told her there was nothing to apologise for since it wasn't intentional. "I'm drow. Sometimes, it's hard for me to control my temper, even though my emotions were tempered in the monasteries," she explained.

"Really, Vhaidra, it is ok," he replied, not wanting to tell her that he could no longer see out of his left eye.

CHAPTER IX
ENTER THE EVIL EYE

After dinner, they had a long, uneventful hike through the caverns. They carried on until suppertime with no sight of the goblin shaman. So, they made camp in a cavern which had a pool of deep water in the middle. Everyone except for Dionysios took turns bathing in the water while others looked the other direction. This time, Elder Dionysios was not allowed to stand watch alone since he was most vulnerable. Vhaidra took four hours, then Ti'erra took the next three hours, and Nikodemos took the last two hours.

DAY 91

Thankfully, nothing happened that night. In the morning, they awoke to light coming in the cavern. They were only one room away from being back outside! They laughed at their fortune and prepared breakfast. Then, they packed up for the short jaunt to the outside, when all of a sudden, it became dark again.

Vhaidra and Ti'erra yelled out, "Ogre!" as an ogre entering the cave was the cause of the sudden darkness. In no time at all, Nikodemos and Dionysios found themselves being punched to the far wall of the room.

"Are you ok, Elder?"

"Don't worry about me, Nikodemos, get to work with your sword!"

"I will, Elder, but you need to show me how to use it better when we get to a city."

"Yes, Nikodemos," he muttered, "Now, remember to watch for my signals!"

Nikodemos charged towards the ogre but was hit by Vhaidra's flying body, which the ogre had picked up and thrown at him.

"Are you ok, dear?" Nikodemos asked.

"Yes, but by the Dark Mother, he will not be for long!" she angrily sputtered.

The ogre picked up Ti'erra, lifting her over his head and looked at her, opening his mouth.

"Wizard, are you going to let him look up my skirt like this?" she asked.

Dionysios began to chant, enraged that Ti'erra felt her modesty was being violated.

Vhaidra threw daggers at the monster's back while Ti'erra raised her greathammer and gave a nasty blow to the ogre's nose.

Dionysios finished chanting, and the water between him and the ogre turned to thick blood. He signalled a plan of attack to the hypodiakonos.

Nikodemos ran behind the monster and cut both of his Achilles' tendons. Then, he went in front and shield-bashed him in the face, causing the ogre to fall head-first, into the water that had turned into blood.

Ti'erra was able to slam her greathammer into the ogre's wrist, breaking the tendons and enabling her to escape, as the monster screamed in pain and fell from multiple simultaneous attacks.

Vhaidra asked in an accusatory manner, "What is that supposed to do, Elder?" pointing to the pool of blood.

"It is living blood; it will hold him in place until he dies," the elder explained.

While the ogre was upside down in the deep pool of water turned to blood, Nikodemos hacked at one calf, while Ti'erra bashed the other calf muscle with her hammer. The ogre looked like he was trying to get out of the pool, but he could not.

"Stop attacking it!" Vhaidra commanded, changing her tone.

"Why?" both Ti'erra and Nikodemos asked.

Vhaidra explained, "This is living blood, the monster will not escape. No reason to damage your weapons to break its bones. Let's go."

"But don't you like to keep beating up our enemies even after they die, Monk?" asked the dwelf.

"Not this time. We are going!" replied the drow, pointing towards the exit.

The group headed out and saw the sun. All were happy to be back in the sunlight, save for Vhaidra. She had appreciated the time in the dark and being underground but needed to get everyone out of there.

Not far away was a city called *Lechaeum*. When they got there, they each went to different shops to spend their collected treasure, save for the elder who did not purchase anything for himself. Instead, he went along to the shops with Nikodemos.

Vhaidra had been saving her treasure from all of her adventures thus far. Now, it was time to discreetly spend it all. Unfortunately, being a despised drow, she was charged higher prices than humans. She could have killed the shopkeepers over such unfairness, but she did not want to cause trouble for Hypo. She bought a huge blue velvet bag that was tied together with a rope. When the rope was loosened, it actually looked like a cape for a giant-sized creature. She filled the bag with sea salt that she purchased. She then bought two scimitars, both made of wood with blades coated in diamond, while their hilts and handles were coated in precious coral. This would help disintegrate the undead and increase the minimum damage of each hit. She next bought a giant-sized wooden circlet encrusted with sixteen enchanted *aquamarine* gemstones. She finally bought two spell scrolls and a spell magnifying necklace made of bone and leather. This took longer than she liked, as the shopkeepers had a hard time with her accent, unlike her friends who were used to it.

Elder Dionysios and Hypodiakonos Nikodemos found the city's episkopos and gave ten per cent of their treasure to him. *Episkopos Valentinos* had greatly admired and revered the elder and gave him a powerful relic, the *Budding Staff of Harun*. Nikodemos was surprised how good Ti'erra's intuition was about the elder getting a miraculous staff! The pair prayed with Episkopos Valentinos of Lechaeum for an hour, and then, the hypodiakonos and the elder went to the agreed-upon inn.

At the inn, Ti'erra was showing off her new *seashell* armour. The elder paid for three rooms – one for him and Nikodemos, one for Ti'erra and one for Vhaidra. Because of his great schema, he was generally treated with respect wherever he went, unlike Vhaidra. So, he was in charge of purchasing the rooms to get the best price.

Elder Dionysios and Hypodiakonos Nikodemos worked on sword and shield skills while Ti'erra drank copious amounts of *ale* in the inn's tavern. After a few hours, she came up to the men's room and pounded on the door. She was slurring so much that neither man could understand her. They helped her to her room and put her to bed. The elder changed her clothes without looking at her naked body.

Meanwhile, Nikodemos knocked on Vhaidra's door, but there was no answer. He wondered where she was. She was actually back at the dungeon entrance that they had exited from and was carefully using her acid cloud spell to dissolve the ogre's skin and muscle, one limb at a time. To get all the bones, she had to take off her clothes and dive into the blood that had returned to the water and get the upper body out of the soot at the bottom of the deep water. After all the skin, tendons, and muscle were dissolved from the acid spells, she cleaned each bone meticulously. She then set them in the sun, rubbed with salt to dry. When all the bones were dry, she washed herself in the water, dried off with the velvet cape-bag, put her clothes back on, and placed all the bones in the bag, placing the circlet she bought on the dead ogre's skull. She also put the leather-sheathed swords and the necklace in the bag. It was heavy, but the magickal jacinth in her armour gave her a boost in her strength.

When she got to the inn late that night, she inquired about her room and took the bag with her. The innkeeper was not happy that the elder had bought a room for a dark elf. There, she stayed up all night reading and studying the scrolls that she had bought.

DAY 92

When Nikodemos woke up, he went and knocked on Vhaidra's door. Still no answer. Unbeknownst to him, she had just slipped into her elven reverie. He went back and had breakfast with the other two adventurers. Then, he went and practised swordsmanship with the elder while Ti'erra nursed her hangover. He was clearly upset that Vhaidra had been ignoring his knocks. At the elder's urging, the cleric went to get his eye checked out by a local doctor of their faith. The doctor had just recently moved to the city, according to Episkopos Valentinos.

Doctor Jerjis confirmed that the eye was dead. It would never work again. Nikodemos began to weep.

The doctor told him not to cry and that he could help since they were of the same faith of The Way. But it would be at a high price. He brought out a black silk bag and showed them an *enchanted ruby eye*. It would allow him to see and even shoot fire from the eye. The downside? He would have to cut out the old eye and replace it with the enchanted ruby eye while Nikodemos was awake. But, as soon as the enchanted ruby eye was placed in his empty eye socket, the nerves would fuse to it, and the pain would be gone.

The cleric figured it was worth the temporary pain as he had been feeling pain ever since the injury. The elder was not so sure. Nikodemos chugged a pain potion and started chanting a prayer of concentration. Even though he was hesitant about this procedure, the elder promised to pay the doctor with his share of treasure if it worked. Doctor Jerjis strapped down the cleric, asked the elder to say a prayer, took out a spoon, and plucked out the old eye, causing Nikodemos to scream in terror. The doctor quickly placed the enchanted ruby eye in, and as promised, the pain stopped immediately.

"Doctor, I still can't see."

"Give it a minute. Patience, patient."

Slowly, the world on his left side came into his line of vision, although it was blurry and red. A minute later, the view was crisp and started gaining other colours. Then, the eye shot fire out and burned the doctor to a crisp.

"Elder, help me!" Nikodemos cried.

The fire was shooting out of his eye, setting fires all over the office. The elder told Nikodemos to chant his prayers and then, closed his eye. Nikodemos did as he was instructed, and the fire slowed and then stopped just before he closed it. The elder did a chant and put out the flames. He searched for a disposal bag and placed the body of the doctor in it, finding an amulet of a jet fist around his neck.

"Oh no, oh no, oh no, what are we going to do now, Elder Dionysios?"

"We're going to have to get you to practice using this eye too. Let's go practice at the dungeon exit we came out of," The elder suggested. The hypodiakonos agreed.

"I killed him, I killed him, I killed him!" Nikodemos screamed.

The elder was eerily calm and told the Cleric that they would discuss this once they got out of town. Now was neither the time nor the place.

Vhaidra had arisen from her reverie, swearing that she heard the scream of her Hypo. She ran to his door, and there was no answer, so she broke the door down. No one was there, and there was no sign of malice. She got dressed and went downstairs to get a meal in the tavern before returning to studying her scrolls.

Outside the city, the Elder told Nikodemos that this death was not his fault and that their God would not hold this against him. However, according to their tradition, he could never be a presbyteros after this. Nikodemos understood. He was starting to think he would be a hypodiakonos for life. They buried the body of Doctor Jerjis and said the *funeral rites* for the deceased doctor.

The male adventurers were going to practice using the eye on the dead ogre but were surprised it was gone. So, instead, the elder had the cleric practice using the eye to hit targets, then varying intensity of attacks, and finally, using it to draw a line around the elder. It took all day, and he was nervous, but Nikodemos mastered the eye very quickly. Or so he thought.

All four met at the inn's tavern for dinner. Vhaidra cried when she saw her Hypo's eye. "Did I make your eye turn all red?"

"Vhaidra, I told you not to worry. Your hair whip accidentally killed my eye, but I got a replacement that gives me full vision back."

"And then some," added the elder.

"I'm so, so sorry, Hypo."

"I told you not to worry," he placated her.

"I think it looks cool, Cleric!" Ti'erra chimed in. "It matches your dragon scale armour!"

After dinner, Vhaidra excused herself, saying she had things to attend to. The males went to their room and saw their damaged door and complained to the innkeeper. He had it repaired immediately, apologising profusely. The elder and hypodiakonos searched their room but saw no other signs of foul play.

Ti'erra came over, and she asked why Vhaidra had been so distant since they came to Lechaeum. Nikodemos did not know why, but the elder suggested patience. So, the three went out and did battle practice throughout the afternoon. Ti'erra soon learned that her seashell armour was not of practical use, when it cracked almost immediately during battle practice, cutting her when it shattered and causing the elder to run and go get her clothing from the inn.

CHAPTER X
THE END OF THE BEGINNING

Elder Dionysios returned from their inn at Lechaeum with Ti'erra's all of their belongings and Vhaidra in tow. The elder was carrying a giant bag on his budding rod.

Since Ti'erra was naked, and he wanted to continue his training, Nikodemos had blindfolded himself and was trying to hit or block rocks that she hit towards him with her greathammer.

Vhaidra growled at Ti'erra being naked in the presence of her Hypo. She announced, "The elder was tipped off that the *Jet Fist Cult* was in Lechaeum, looking for us. So, it is time to leave."

Then, looking at the elder, Ti'erra asked, "What's in that big bag, Wizard?"

"It's my stuff, get dressed NOW, Ti'erra!" Vhaidra hissed, answering the question for the elder.

Nikodemos took off his blindfold, once that the dwelf had got dressed. The group walked back into the cave entrance that they had previously journeyed in, had dinner, bathed, (except for the Elder, as usual) and rested for the night.

DAY 93

In the morning, they had their breakfast before travelling back to where they had met the goblins. When they entered that room around dinner time, they found that the goblin shaman had returned along with two *hobgoblins*.

The shaman immediately saw them and screamed, pointing at them with his now thawed fingers. He started waving his staff and chanting something. The two hobgoblins instantly went for Vhaidra and Ti'erra, hating elves with a passion.

The elder shouted out, "Kill the shaman first if you can, he is empowering the hobgoblins!"

Vhaidra asked the elder to fling her bag at the hobgoblins. Then, she started chanting. The elder had tried to make the bag hit the monsters, but the bag hit the ceiling, bounced off and landed behind the hobgoblins. The two monsters stopped, looked at the bag that missed them and then, laughed. Dionysios began to chant.

At the same time, Nikodemos used his shield to block the magick missile that the shaman threw at them. Then, he hit one hobgoblin with his greatsword while Ti'erra hit the other with her greathammer. Vhaidra finished her chant with, "...arise *Skeletogre!*" and out of the bag arose the skeleton of the ogre they battled, wearing the bag as a cape and wearing the wooden circlet and bone necklace Vhaidra had bought earlier. Skeletogre was also equipped with the two scimitars Vhaidra had purchased.

Nikodemos and Ti'erra were shocked. The Cleric ran away from the hobgoblin he had attacked and used his sword to cut the hands off of the shaman, and Ti'erra used her hammer to break its neck. Nikodemos went and broke the shaman's staff, throwing it into a nearby fire. He was afraid to use his eye for a fire attack in such close quarters and with his friends nearby. The shaman screamed in pain, somehow still alive, but continued to chant, trying to heal the hobgoblins, his only hope for survival.

Meanwhile, the undead ogre, Skeletogre, had stabbed the two hobgoblins in the back. The elder finished chanting, and a swarm of locusts surrounded the shaman, quickly eating off his flesh and intestines. Elder Dionysios noticed how his own chants seemed even stronger as if the Budding Staff was magnifying the effects of his chants. Vhaidra ran over to the goblin shaman and punched him in his temples, gave him a double-fisted uppercut and then punched him in the jugular veins. Between this and the locust attack, he quickly lost consciousness and died.

Finally, the hobgoblins stopped being healed, so Nikodemos then did his signature Achilles tendon cut on one hobgoblin while Ti'erra used her hammer to break the hip of the other. Then, Skeletogre finished them off with his twin diamond scimitars.

"Monk, that was a great trick!" Ti'erra screamed.

"Thanks. Sorry, I've been such a recluse, but this is what I have been working on. Where to now?"

Ti'erra rolled her die again, and this time, it landed on an eight. So, after dinner, they took the eighth passageway to the right. At Vhaidra's urging, Skeletogre led the way.

CHAPTER XI
FAITH LOST, LOVE FOUND

"I thought you had been avoiding me because of the kiss we shared when I saved you from the rust monsters," Nikodemos whispered to Vhaidra.

"Oh, no, not at all, Hypo. When we stopped the ogre, I had felt my qi strengthening. I knew I wanted to take my *raise undead* spell up a level, and this ogre would be a perfect specimen. So, I bought this equipment, bought a *qi spell,* allowing me to raise an undead giant, and another qi spell, allowing me to raise a skeleton for one to two full days without draining my own power. Studying the qi spells, I figured out how to combine them, and now, I can raise Skeletogre for up to forty-eight hours, and after he falls, I can immediately raise him again."

"Oh, that is impressive. Have you considered buying him armour?"

"I would not give him metal due to my fear of rust monsters. So, I think it might be pointless."

"Understood," he replied, deciding not to press the issue.

"Sorry, I have been ignoring you, Hypo. Let me make that up to you now," Vhaidra added, giving him a kiss.

"Thank you, dear," he said with a smile.

"My pleasure, Hypo."

The path they had taken had an eerie glow, almost a low-level moonlight glow. What was even eerier was that there were no monsters along this path. They walked for a full day and saw no signs of life until a cavern where they stopped at for supper and rest. There, in the middle of the cavern was a beautiful drow *priestess* hung from a jagged stalactite by a noose.

Vhaidra climbed up the body and saw her *amethyst* symbol, "She is a priestess of the House Godeep! They are, or at least, they were a very powerful house." No visible marks showed the cause of death. Vhaidra slit the dead priestess' neck, and blood poured out. "It appears she only just recently died, within the last day or so, and likely by powerful magicks."

Vhaidra removed the dead drow's house symbol and cape of invisibility. This would be a very good house to pretend to be part of, should she have to pretend to be a slaver of her friends. She now had two house pendants, which could be good, giving her options depending on who they may meet.

"Monk, can we get rid of that bleeding corpse? I don't like sleeping under such a decoration," Ti'erra whined.

"Skeletogre, dig a hole," Vhaidra commanded.

The skeleton of the ogre did as he was ordered.

"Skeletogre, remove this body."

He did as she commanded.

"Skeletogre, bury the body."

He did as she commanded.

"Skeletogre, watch the entrances to this area."

He did as she commanded.

The team supped and rested for the night. When Vhaidra arose from her elven reverie, she found Skeletogre had collapsed. So, she gathered his bones and put him back in the cape-bag along with his weapons and circlet. She placed the bag on Elder Dionysios' Budding Staff so that he could carry it, as per his previous wish to volunteer in this task.

DAY 94

The next day, they continued until they exited into an ancient forest. It was evening by then, and the sun had already set. A full moon was rising. To the left, there was a huge temple, almost completely hidden behind the tall trees. If it had not been for the fact that the temple was glowing with the same glow of moonlight on the path that they took, the adventurers would have missed it completely. Cautiously, the four approached the temple, opened the doors, and stepped in.

As the doors shut behind them, two things happened at once.

First, a group of perhaps twenty drow rushed them, and second, Hypodiakonos Nikodemos' Armour of The Ancient of Days had completely disappeared. Once again, he was barefoot and wearing only the red dragon scale armour. He was sure he was going to die. He said a quick prayer.

CHAPTER XII
EVIL AND THE MOON

"Welcome to the *Temple of the Dark Maiden,*" the surrounding Drow greeted them.

"*The Dark Maiden*, the Spider Queen's eldest daughter?" Vhaidra asked.

"One and the same, dear sister," replied one of the many drow, "Do you not worship her?"

"No, I do not worship her, nor do I any longer worship her vile mother, the Spider Queen, or any other Goddess."

"Nevertheless, you are welcome here, sister, for here, you have escaped the evil of the Dark Mother."

Vhaidra could not believe it. A huge gathering of drow who did not worship the Spider Queen? She was weary but excited at the same time.

"Who are you and your companions, dear sister, and why do you find yourself here?" another dark elf asked her.

"I am Vhaidra of the House..." she reached for one of the house symbols she had and then thought better of it, as perhaps, members of those houses were here, "...of no house. This human cleric is Hypo..., or rather, Hypodiakonos Nikodemos, the half-elf is Ti'erra, and the hooded one is Elder Dionysios. We are all from the city of Sicyon."

The drow invited them to come, enjoy the setting, "Please, come in and enjoy our food, items for trade, our music, and most importantly... *dancing*!"

The four adventurers came further in, and Vhaidra noticed that Hypo was very excitable, talking to the elder.

"What is wrong, Hypo?" she asked.

"As soon as the doors shut to the temple, the whole Armour of The Ancient of Days disappeared!" he explained.

"I think because we are in the realm of another God; the connection to The Ancient of Days' Armour has been severed!" the elder added.

"By the Dark Mother!" she exclaimed.

"I hope it will reappear once we leave, but it appears we have no need for shields, swords, and armour right now anyway," the elder smiled.

"Let me ask around." Vhaidra noticed the temple was mostly a place of worship, but on the sides, there were shops with medicine, armour, clothing, jewellery, musical instruments, books, and more.

A group of drow came up to the three non-drow visitors and started to ask them about Vhaidra. One noticed Nikodemos' eye and cried out, "*The Evil Eye!* The Evil Eye! The Evil Eye!"

Another drow came running up, and Nikodemos felt the eye getting hot.

"Help! It is burning me! Oh, no! Runaway!" he cried out as the eye started shooting out fire everywhere. Most of the nimble drow were doing a great job using their acrobatic skills to avoid the fiery blasts, and they were unsure if they should kill the human. After all, he was now a guest in the temple. To kill him here would be a grave sacrilege.

After the blast killed one drow, who was not paying attention to the human, but carefully looking at some other dark elf clergy and making notes, Vhaidra ran over to defend her Hypo, sensing the desire of some to kill him.

"Hypo! Stop your eye!"

"I can't, Vhaidra. It has taken complete control!"

She slapped him to get him to calm down and yelled, "Try to shut your eye!"

"Ok, I will," he replied. Then, he cried out in pain as the eye burned his eyelids clean off. Thankfully, the wound was instantly cauterised.

A five feet and ten inches tall, the naked *priestess* of the Dark Maiden with light silver hair swirling around her body, acting as clothing, calmly walked to them in the air, holding a moonstone encrusted hand mirror, and reflected the fiery beams back into the red eye. She walked up and pushed the mirror directly up against the eye, causing it to be destroyed. Nikodemos cried in pain! The hypodiakonos grabbed for his missing sword in vain.

"By the Dark Mother, what did you do to him?" Vhaidra cried out, reaching for her daggers.

"Vhaidra, I destroyed the evil relic that was in his eye socket. Do you know who caused him to lose his original eye?"

"It... it... it was me...," Vhaidra looked at the ground, ashamed but also shocked that this priestess knew her name.

"Do you abuse the human a lot, dear sister?"

"I do not intend to do it. My drow temper just gets the best of me sometimes."

"It sounds like both of you need healing then," the drow priestess replied.

Nikodemos knelt down on the ground, holding his eye socket and crying in pain. Blood was pouring out of his eye socket from the explosion of what the dark elves had called the Evil Eye.

The priestess pulled him up into the air with one hand, and she held Vhaidra's arm with her other hand. She called up an apothecary to join her as she walked through the air to the rose-covered moonstone altar of the Dark Maiden.

They laid the two on the altar; his head to her feet, her head to his feet. The apothecary poured a pain-numbing potion into his eye socket and then tweezed the pieces of the destroyed Evil Eye out. He put all the pieces in a mortar and crushed them with a pestle. He then tilted Nikodemos' head, collected the remaining potion and blood in the mortar, and poured a healing potion into the eye socket. All this time, the priestess was chanting and formed an eye out of pure *moonlight*, turning it into a *blessed moonstone.*

She placed the eye in the empty eye socket and whispered, "It will not be a weapon anymore, and it cannot see either, as your optic nerve has been destroyed, but it will be a symbol of your family's destiny."

"What... what is my destiny?"

"You have already met her. Now, you need to truly get to know her soon-to-be cleansed soul, human."

The priestess continued to chant and lay her hands on Vhaidra. She placed one hand on her face and another on her left bosom. The priestess asked for all the hate and evil that still resided in Vhaidra's heart, mind, spirit, and soul to be purged from her. The priestess was surprised to see how much evil had already been purged from Vhaidra. She had never met a monk who self-purged the Dark Mother from her heart, mind, spirit, and soul before. The tall Drow knew that this monk was very special, indeed. She continued her chant, moving one hand down to her belly, "You are light, you are love, you are whole, you are blessed, you are legend, you are divine..."

A shadow of darkness arose from out of Vhaidra, and the priestess formed this into a stone as well, a *cursed jet stone.* She gave this to the apothecary who crushed it much as he had done with the fragments of the Evil Eye. Vhaidra, for only the briefest fraction of a moment, appeared to have lost her dark-grey skin colour, appearing with a skin tone of the palest high elf, and her clothes transformed to a pure white outfit of a dancer. When the moment passed, she returned to her regular form with her black leather and white bone armour.

The priestess announced to the temple congregants, "Sistren, brethren, please forgive the human. The Evil Eye was in control, and I sense he has no hate or evil in him, only love for our sister, Vhaidra. Please make them and their friends welcome." She then went to speak to the *armourer*.

One of the dark elves approached the priestess and showed her the jet fist amulet that the dead drow had been wearing. The priestess nodded and continued towards the armourer.

She leaned in and whispered to the armourer, "The human had armour of another God until he came in here. This temple has severed his connection as being a *chosen* of that God. Please make for him a great weapon and armour made of dragon bones for his feet, arms, chest, and body. Do not use any metal in its construction, as our sister here has a phobia."

"Yes, *Dark Dancer,*" he replied, bowing, and went to the human, asking to take measurements so that he could properly complete the task he had been given.

"Thank you, priestess!" Vhaidra exclaimed, "What should I call you? Mother? Matron? Mistress?"

"You may call me the Dark Maiden, or the Dark Dancer."

"You are the Goddess herself, not her priestess?"

"Yes, my dear sister, I am the Dark Maiden in the flesh."

Whether Vhaidra worshipped her or not, she knew she should bow. She did a full prostration and said, "Forgive me, Dark Maiden."

Grabbing her hand from the ground and raising her up, the Dark Maiden replied, "You have nothing to ask forgiveness for. You owe me nothing. All your evil in your past is due to my evil mother, the Spider Queen."

"Thank you, Dark Maiden."

"This human, he is the chosen of The Ancient of Days. Stay with him, follow Him and find your destiny."

"Yes, Dark Maiden."

"Please excuse me, Vhaidra. I must attend to other matters. Please feel free to stay here all night... Oh, do try to stop calling on the name of my evil mother. Simply saying any of her many names gives her power, and specifically, power over you!"

"Yes, Dark Maiden, just an unintended habit I've yet to purge."

Vhaidra did another full prostration. She was exhausted and excited at the same time. She looked around; Hypo was talking to the armourer while the elder was engaged in discussion with some other drow. Ti'erra was dancing with others and talking to the Dark Dancer at the same time. Vhaidra decided to go to the shops. She didn't have any gold pieces left, but she knew that if she found something she liked, Hypo would buy it for her. That thought stopped her for a moment. She had never thought of, depending on a male before. This was anathema in the Spider Queen's society. But she embraced it; she liked the feeling of being able to depend on another without fear of betrayal. "So, is this the overworlders' emotion called love?" she asked herself silently. She had thought it to just be a myth.

CHAPTER XIII
DRY DIRT

The party spent the night awake in the temple. Vhaidra, unfortunately, had found nothing she wished to purchase but was able to speak with the Dark Maiden about her future plans for a few minutes before they left. Before the sun started to rise, most of the Drow had returned to their homes. By this time, Nikodemos had been outfitted with dragon bone armour and a dragon bone Yan Yue Dao. He was very happy about this. The elder paid the armourer for the armour, and the group got ready to leave the temple after breakfast.

Vhaidra asked Ti'erra what the Dark Dancer had said to her while she was dancing.

"Oh, Monk, the Goddess said that my dancing was beautiful and that I should never stop dancing. She also said that she and I will meet again in the future in our darkest hour."

"That sounds ominous," Vhaidra replied.

DAY 95

Exiting the temple, Nikodemos found himself in extreme pain. He screamed out in agony, "It's crushing me!"

"By the Dark Moth... what's happening, Hypo?" Vhaidra asked.

The elder understood what was happening and explained, "Now that we have left the temple, the Armour of The Ancient of Days has returned. Since he has outer armour on already, the armours are fighting for space and uniting into one combined armour. This is really miraculous!"

"But it is hurting him. We must cut it off!" she screamed.

"No, this pain is good for him. He must suffer so that he may live," the elder mused.

"Has he not suffered enough?" she asked, horrified to see him suffer yet again.

The armours did combine, just as Dionysios said. The pain caused Nikodemos to collapse. The armour was now *shining bone armour*, but less of a glow came from it, more like a gentle *moonlight* rather than bright sunlight. The shape was somewhat like bones, but not exactly. The double-headed eagle motif remained throughout the pieces, and his weapon was not exactly a Yan Yue Dao and not exactly a greatsword. The shield now appeared more like an energy shield, a part of the gauntlet, but could change in size. What it was... was somewhat unexplainable. Like before, each person would explain the armour, weapon, and shield a little differently, seeing it as they understood it.

After the armours finished merging, Nikodemos was able to stand, even though he remained in pain. Vhaidra helped him both stand and walk. Dionysios led them to a different dungeon entrance which they entered not long after the sun had risen above the trees.

"We will never have anything to do with the Temple of the Dark Maiden ever again!" he exclaimed, rubbing his sore belly.

Vhaidra knew he was wrong, after having talked to Ti'erra, but she kept silent about this.

There they took rest while Skeletogre was summoned to stand guard. When Nikodemos took off his armour, everyone could see the imprint of dragon bones and double-headed eagles on his skin. He was bleeding from his wrists, ankles, the side of his torso, and the crown of his head. Vhaidra took care of his wounds as he fell fast asleep after his evening prayers.

After six hours of rest, everyone was awake and ready to journey after a quick dinner. After many hours of empty rooms, save for the constant flow of trinkets that Ti'erra would find, they finally entered a room with three *dryders*.

"By the Dark Mother! Oops!" Vhaidra shouted, out of habit rather than by any religious allegiance, as Skeletogre ran at the creatures and was instantly bound up in spider silk.

"What's wrong?" Nikodemos asked, wondering if her skeleton was the cause of concern.

"Dryders are immune to poison and most of my spells. It's going to have to be hand-to-hand combat with them." She pulled out two daggers and ran for one of the *half-Drow/half-spider* creatures.

The elder began to chant. Nikodemos ran for another dryder, siding under it and cutting all eight of its legs off with his great weapon. Ti'erra slammed her greathammer into another one's mouth, knocking it backwards. Vhaidra tried to do the same as her Hypo, only to get wrapped up in webbing before she could get more than one leg cut off using her daggers that were really meant for throwing.

The dryder that had caught her in webs approached with its two scimitars as Ti'erra chased her prey. Nikodemos, seeing Vhaidra in trouble, went over and stopped the attack with his great weapon and then, used the same to cut off the legs of the dryder. Before he could check on her, Vhaidra had used her daggers to cut herself free and implant the daggers in the now legless dryder's temples.

The other dryder spun a web to cover Nikodemos just as the elder's chant brought down a storm of fireballs on to the three dryders. Ti'erra hammered down on her prey's head over and over again until it stopped moving, while Vhaidra cut her Hypo free, removed her daggers from the nearest dryder, and did an amazing flip! She then slammed the blades into the heart and neck of the other legless dryder. Next, she cut Skeletogre free and made sure that Ti'erra had killed the third dryder, by beating it profusely and ensuring that it was not moving.

When they were all confirmed kills, she built a fire and expertly roasted the spider leg meat from the non-poisoned dryders. None of the others had ever eaten a spider before, but found it quite delicious, save for the elder, who did not eat meat.

"I thought drow worshipped *spiders*, Monk?" Ti'erra asked.

"Well, we think highly of them, but we also venerate the *matrons* of high houses, and we kill them too. Most drow have no sentimental thoughts, so eating a spider is not unheard of in some cities. Me, not being a worshipper of the Spider Queen anymore, I have no special affinity for spiders."

"Who do you worship, Monk?"

"Nobody!" she curtly replied. "I only depend on myself... ... and my friends for survival and good luck."

"I do hope that one day you will see the good in worshipping The Ancient of Days," Nikodemos added.

"I see the good that you get from worshipping your God, Hypo. I'm not sure that I would get any good from it. Would he even want worship from a drow?"

"He wishes to be worshipped by all whom he created."

"I'm not sure he created drow, Hypo," she smirked.

The elder pulled him to the side and told him in a quiet voice not to worry himself about converting her, "It may come in time, and your incessant pushing her towards The Way could, in reality, push her away."

"Ti'erra, who do you worship?" Vhaidra quickly asked.

"I worship whatever God I am in the lands of. In the *moonstone temple,* I worshipped the Dark Dancer with your fellow drow. When the wizard and cleric do their morning, evening, and meal prayers, I follow along, worshipping their God, The Ancient of Days. When I was working in the club, I worshipped the Jet Fist Cults' God, Lord Kajne. Growing up, I worshipped Shakti in my village. She is the shining

Goddess of gaiety, romance, and dance. Worshipping in that drow temple reminded me somewhat of those days."

Vhaidra thought that maybe Ti'erra was right to worship Hypo's and Dionysios' God. They were all more likely to be protected by this Ancient of Days if they all worshipped him together. So, tonight, she listened to their evening prayers in a prostrate position like the others before they rested for the night.

CHAPTER XIV
THE ILLUSIONS AND THE ODYSSEY

DAY 96

After breakfast in the morning, the group looked for a way out. There was only the way they entered. Vhaidra insisted this was wrong. Dryders would not just sit in a cul-de-sac. There had to be a way out.

She instructed the dwelf to start hitting walls with her greathammer, and she began to look for switches. Nikodemos and the elder also looked around. Skeletogre just walked back and forth, but inadvertently, hit a hidden switch, opening a hole in the middle of the room where he had stood. Skeletogre fell a long distance, disappearing from sight.

"Noooooooooo!" Vhaidra cried out, as she had spent so much time, money, and energy in getting this skeleton to serve her on a full-time basis. As she wept, she saw a switch and pulled it, opening a wall to the left. At the same time, Ti'erra broke a wall to the right.

"Which way should we go?" asked Nikodemos.

Ti'erra reached into her bag of dice and pulled out a gold coin with a *crown* on one side and an *eagle* on the other. "Crown up we go left, wings up we go right," she said, flipping the coin in the air. It landed crown up, so they headed left.

Vhaidra was comforted by her Hypo as they journeyed on.

After many hours, they realised they had connected to a newly opened passage to the number eight tunnel they had been in days before. As such, they returned to the room where they had started this morning and had lunch before going right. Going right for many hours, they ended at a pool at a dead end. They took turns bathing and then again returned to their original starting place.

"Perhaps we need to go down?" Ti'erra inquired.

"Mayhap, but how do we all go down? The pit is deep," Vhaidra replied.

The elder began to chant and levitated them all up into the air and then, slowly down into the pit. They landed in the middle of a massacre.

Skeletogre was in pieces, and along with him were three dead *brain floggers*, robe wearing creatures that looked like humanoids with octopi over their skulls, cut into many pieces. Nikodemos immediately grabbed his holy salt and threw it in a cruciform manner on the heads of each dead brain flogger, not wanting to chance that they were able to feast on their brains. Ti'erra also hit their heads with her greathammer, to freeze and smash them.

Vhaidra chanted, raised Skeletogre back to his undead life, and gave him a big hug. She suggested that they stop here for supper and rest. Thankfully, Skeletogre, being mindless, had been given an advantage in this fight. Had it been the four living members of their party, they likely would have fallen to these treacherous foes!

"I sense much *evil* around here," Elder Dionysios murmured.

Vhaidra recommended that tonight they sleep in their armour and have two on night watch along with Skeletogre, just to be careful. The elder chanted for a circle of protection while Nikodemos and Ti'erra slept. Vhaidra just listened while sitting next to her Hypo.

Although they were not all asleep at once, at one point during the night, after the elder had gone to sleep, they found themselves, save for Skeletogre, stuck in their worst nightmare possible, due to a nearby *dream larva.* For the elder and Ti'erra, it was a nightmare of being mocked for being bastards, for Vhaidra, it was a dream of rust monsters attacking her, and for Nikodemos, it was watching his family members die and telling him it was his fault. It took Skeletogre a long time while marching on guard in a circle around the party, but he finally figured out there was a hidden enemy near, and engaged the dream larva, killing it after many rounds of combat. The party was so weakened by the attack, that they were confused, and all rested at the same time. Once again, Skeletogre's mindlessness had saved them.

DAY 97

The group came to consciousness at the same time, finding themselves caught inside Skeletogre's bag. Vhaidra cut a small hole with one of her daggers and saw that they were hung high over a raging bonfire below them. And who was around the fire?

Three small lizard-men called *kobolds* and an undead necromancer called a *lich,* dancing around the fire and chanting. Things were going from bad to worse quickly!

CHAPTER XV
LICHING THE KOBOLD

Vhaidra whispered to the others to tell them what she saw.

She thought the best thing was for Elder Dionysios and her to each launch a spell, then for her to throw daggers at the kobolds before Hypo and Ti'erra dropped down and used their great weapons against the undead lich. But first, she would raise Skeletogre, who was just a pile of bones on the ground below.

The group agreed and quietly, she called for Skeletogre to arise. The skeleton arose without his bag for a cape and started to attack the kobolds.

She had hoped that he would attack the lich since the enchanted diamond blades of his scimitars would be great against an undead lich.

The elder chanted and created an earthquake under the bonfire and the four creatures. Vhaidra followed that up with an acid cloud and then, cut open the bag fully, throwing her daggers and preparing herself for a long fall. But Dionysios used his levitation chant, and they slowly descended to the ground, where the four monsters along with Skeletogre were on the ground due to the tremors.

Ti'erra and Nikodemos tried to attack the lich but found that he was covered by a magickal shield.

Vhaidra and Skeletogre were successfully battling the kobolds when Nikodemos came up with a plan, "Prepare to hit his left hip, Ti'erra."

"Affirmative, Cleric," she replied.

Hypodiakonos Nikodemos then threw holy water in a cruciform shape, which opened up a hole in his magickal shield.

"NOW!" he shouted.

Ti'erra had her greathammer cocked back and swung full force at the lich's hip just as he shot a fireball at Nikodemos, surrounding him in fire. He protected his face and hands with his shield and was happy that his newly merged armour seemed to be flame-resistant.

The lich broke in two from the freezing action and force of the blow from Ti'erra's greathammer, and his shield went down. He began a new chant, using the energies of the now-dead kobolds.

The elder, realising this lich was a *necromancer*, started his own chant, a *blessing*.

Normally, a blessing would help someone, but in this case, it hurt the necromancer and made him feel *fear*.

The lich struck out at Vhaidra, seeing her running towards him with her fists ready for mortal combat.

The lifeforce-stealing blast made Vhaidra feel weak, and she collapsed where she was, hitting the ground hard. Skeletogre ran past his downed mistress and started hitting the lich with his diamond-coated blades. Nikodemos, once the fire around him had subsided, escaping with only a lightly burned face and hands, ran over to pick up Vhaidra and to take her to safety.

"You've got to break his jaws, his fingers, and his arm bones!" Dionysios yelled to Ti'erra.

"On it, Wizard!" she shouted, doing as she was instructed.

However, the necromancer was now even stronger, having taken the energies of his dead companions as well as stealing health from Vhaidra. He put his body together and began to chant again.

Ti'erra swung at him, but he teleported. The elder was now the closest one to the necromancer, so he jabbed his Budding Staff into the lich's ribs and flung him towards Ti'erra. Once again, the elder's aim was awful, and the lich hit the ceiling before dropping in front of the dwelf. Ti'erra swung her greathammer and shattered the monster's already-cracked rib cage.

Its skull popped off and landed near the kobolds, and he chanted again, raising them back to undead life.

Nikodemos wrapped *holy basil* around Vhaidra, gave her holy water to drink, and anointed her with holy oil as her heartbeat started to fade.

Vhaidra struggled to whisper, "Don't worry about me now, Hypo, kill the necromancer and his spells die with him. This is how *necromancy* works."

Nikodemos stood up with much anger and shouted, "Leave the lich skull to me!" as he ran towards the undead creatures.

Off to the side, Ti'erra smashed all of the bones of the headless body of the lich, focusing first on his hands and arms, as she had been told. Skeletogre fought the undead kobolds. Nikodemos jammed his greatsword into the mouth of the lich, twisting it, and breaking the bottom jaw off. Then, he picked up the skull and smashed it against a rock until there were only shards left. His hand was left bleeding.

Elder Dionysios called down fire again and this, along with Skeletogre's attacks, permanently destroyed the undead kobolds.

Vhaidra stood up, re-energised with the necromancer dead, and asked the team to bring all the fragments of the creatures together. They collected them carefully, and she used her acid cloud to disintegrate all of them.

There were wounds to bind, healing potions to drink, and breakfast to be eaten before they could go on.

CHAPTER XVI
THE WICKED WITCH OF THE WHAT?

The group walked all day, having stopped for dinner earlier, and nothing had changed. The long tunnel they were walking down did not change, and they never got anywhere. Vhaidra went back to the elder and whispered to him, "I feel strong magicks holding us here. I think we have not gone anywhere."

"I was getting the same feeling. What do you think we should do?"

"I am going to keep walking but chant a darkness spell so that whoever has us trapped, wherever we are, cannot see us. Then, we can secretly make a plan."

"Hmm, maybe if you do that and I call down the Uncreated Light from the heavens, the opposing forces can help break us free?"

"Or, at least, weaken whatever is holding us in this place that is not really a place."

"Ok, let's begin."

Vhaidra brought darkness all around them and told each member of their party to get ready to throw their weapons as hard as they could. Then, Elder Dionysios called down the Uncreated Light. Vhaidra yelled for everyone to throw their weapons, and as she and the elder suspected, the weapons, along with the darkness and the Uncreated Light, destroyed the dimensional ball that they had been trapped in. Vhaidra could see the source, a powerful drow priestess, *Irriina of House Tekken'duis.*

They were in far worse trouble than Vhaidra could have ever guessed.

The light had blinded the priestess, so everyone ran to get their weapons that they had thrown. Unfortunately, for Nikodemos, after he retrieved his great weapon, the priestess had been able to catch him with her five-snake whip. The whip held him tight with his arms bound behind him, as the living whip tightened, slowly squeezing the breath out of him.

She shouted at Vhaidra, "You dare have feelings for this short-life human pet? I watched you and him. You made me sick! You are an abomination to all drow everywhere!"

Vhaidra prepared her daggers for throwing, but the priestess used the whip to grab and use her Hypo as a literal human shield while she opened a huge dark portal with her staff. Seeing how helpless the monk was, she just laughed and threw the cleric through the portal and walked through it herself cackling, "You'll never see your pet again, my pretty!"

Vhaidra looked at the others, and they knew what they must do. They all ran and jumped through the portal before it could close. They landed with a hard thud and looked around. Vhaidra led them through the path to another room where Nikodemos was in a sword fight with a person who looked somewhat like a darker version of him. Oddly, their swords never hit one another, or one another's shields. It was as if they could read one another's minds or had the exact same style of fighting technique, and as such, could completely evade one another's attacks.

The drow priestess could not be seen anywhere. But they were not alone either.

CHAPTER XVII
THROUGH THE PORTAL TO THE SHADES

DAY 197

Unbeknownst to them, the portal not only took them to another place but took them to another time! One hundred days into the future to be exact. Vhaidra noticed that her Hypo's beard and hair were now noticeably longer. Dionysios noticed his beard had grown, and Ti'erra's hair had grown as well. The whole group, save for Vhaidra and Skeletogre, felt sick to their stomachs. The portal was a bumpy ride and had caused all kinds of havoc on their digestive systems.

Fighting with Nikodemos was a very dark-skinned human cleric, Alric, who had long grey hair and a matching long beard. Alric wore weathered *copper dragon scale armour* with *dark plate armour* over it. The plate armour seemed to suck-in the light around him. They seemed perfectly matched, as neither could get a hit on one another. But the two clerics were not alone.

There was a heavily plate-armoured male *orc* lich, an *undead necromancer* named *Sudagog*, who had magickal control over his possibly pregnant, short, pale, submissive slave high elf named *Feyrdryl*. The slave wore an impractical *metal bikini* with enchanted *amethyst* all over it and had ankle-length midnight-black hair. Sudagog held a large *serrated dagger*, and Feyrdryl had twin scimitars with enchanted *topaz*.

There was a male *half-ogre wizard* named *Blossthus* who wore only black cloth boots, gloves, and a mask covering his nose and mouth. He held a solid enchanted *jade* Yan Yue Dao in one hand and in his other hand, he held the hand of a small dwelf female rogue. This rogue was a half-drow and half-*duergar* or *grey dwarf* named *El'ienna* who wore a *copper dragon scale bikini* with enchanted *pearls* on the strings tying it together. She also had long, *copper dragon scale bracers*, *thigh-high boots*, and *throwing axes* for weapons.

The friends were not happy to be fighting another necromancer. One had been enough, but this looked to be possibly even more powerful, with much stouter backup!

The elder whispered instructions. He used hand signals to notify Nikodemos of their plans. Vhaidra repeated the directions to Skeletogre in quiet tones. Everyone realised who their nemesis was in this weird world. While Nikodemos fought Alric, Skeletogre advanced to attack Sudagog, Vhaidra faced Feyrdryl, Dionysios chanted to begin his spell for Blossthus and Ti'erra raised her hammer as she ran towards El'ienna.

But it was all a ruse. As soon as they started running, Nikodemos ran backwards and slammed his greatsword into the lower spine of Sudagog, while Ti'erra hit him in the pelvis. Vhaidra threw her poisoned daggers at the bare-chested Blossthus while Dionysios called the pit of vipers to attack the half-ogre as well. Meanwhile, Skeletogre was dual scimitar fighting with Feyrdryl.

Next, the team tricked Alric into running to where El'ienna was throwing her axes. His armour protected him, but it threw both of them into a quick state of confusion. This moment was planned, and Skeletogre disengaged from Feyrdryl and stabbed El'ienna through the back with his two scimitars. Meanwhile, Nikodemos grabbed Alric's arms from behind, which caused a massive unplanned explosion.

The two armours were opposites. Alric wore the *Armour of Asmodeus*; Nikodemos wore the Armour of The Ancient of Days. When the armours hit each other, they cancelled each other out like matter and antimatter. Every piece of the cleric's armour hit the opposite piece due to the way Nikodemos grabbed him. It knocked both clerics out completely.

Thankfully for the adventurers, it did not take long for Blossthus and El'ienna to die due to their lack of armour. However, while Vhaidra called an acid cloud down on Sudagog's skull, and Dionysios called down a fireball attack, Feyrdryl's attacks broke Skeletogre apart.

While Vhaidra went to go check on her Hypo, Ti'erra finished crushing Sudagog's body and then went to war with Feyrdryl, who was inexplicably acting confused. Even in her confusion, the two were equally matched until Dionysios used his Budding Staff to hit the high elf at the base of her skull, knocking her out.

"You're my hero, Wizard!" Ti'erra cried out, jumping into his arms, "Do you think we are to be a couple like those otherworldly versions of us?"

"Most certainly not," he exclaimed, rolling his eyes and setting her down on the floor as he walked over towards the now-dead Blossthus. He thought to himself, '*This was almost too easy. Things are not quite what they appear, I fear.*'

She giggled and ran away, checking on the monk and the cleric.

"Monk, is the cleric dead?"

"No, he is just knocked out, like the other cleric, over there," she replied, pointing to Alric, who was starting to wake.

Ti'erra ran over and smashed the face of Alric over and over again, killing him brutally. "Monk, this cleric is not just knocked out!" she laughed.

Nikodemos woke up in pain and with a massive headache. "Not again!" he complained.

"What, Hypo?" Vhaidra asked.

"My armour... gone again!"

"I think it is gone for good, this time," Elder Dionysios sadly explained as he approached. He had gone over to Blossthus and removed his boots, gloves, mask and Yan Yue Dao, bringing them over to Vhaidra. "Do you think you can alter these clothes to fit him?"

Vhaidra nodded affirmatively and got on to the task, while Ti'erra made supper and the elder tended to Nikodemos. Ti'erra claimed the dragon scale bikini for herself and put it on under her leather after washing it thoroughly. She put the boots and bracers in her bag of holding.

"That will hardly protect you, Ti'erra!"

"I know, Monk, but I think it is pretty, so I will wear it to protect my womanly parts."

Vhaidra just rolled her eyes.

No one realised that the pregnant high elf female was now conscious, still holding her dual blades and watching the scene with her eyes squinted, feigning to be dead.

"How are we going to get back?" Nikodemos asked.

The elder handed Nikodemos the solid enchanted jade Yan Yue Dao. "The Ancient of Days will provide, Young Hypodiakonos, just like this weapon you obtained. He will provide."

CHAPTER XVIII
FRIEND OR FOE?

That night, when Nikodemos took off his dragon scale armour, he, and everyone else, realised that he had the imprints on his body from the Armour still, but now there was a faint glow coming from those marks. His hair was now long and thick enough to cover the glowing marks of the double-headed eagle on either side of his head, but they could be seen when he combed his lengthening hair.

His arms and legs were another story, even though they were covered with a dark layer of hair. His forearms both had visible dragon bone and double-headed eagles imprinted and glowing, and on the back of his palms were a cruciform shape. His lower legs were the same way except for the crisscross marks on his knees. His chest and back also had the dragon bone and double-eagle imprints.

He hit himself in the places where the glowing images appeared, and it felt like human flesh over armour, but he decided to keep this to himself, not understanding how internalised armour could possibly help him. He decided to keep wearing the dragon scale armour that Vhaidra had made him, regardless of what had happened.

After a while, his curiosity ceased, and he fell asleep as Vhaidra played with his growing beard. (He had not shaved since she had shaved him one hundred forty-seven days ago.)

Vhaidra thought of cutting the beard again but decided against it. She had grown used to his appearance and now, found something attractive about this bestial face fur.

Feyrdryl was so thirsty after faking death while the elder had buried some of the bodies under stones. So, she decided to try something. She waited until it was Vhaidra's watch, then she whispered, "Save me, sister!"

Vhaidra ran from beside her Hypo to the high elf with her daggers out.

"Save me, sister!" the high elf whispered again.

"Why would I save you, high elf scum?"

"Water, please. I am pregnant, and I know how to get you out of here."

Vhaidra knew this was important information, so she got water for Feyrdryl and asked her why she should trust a high elf.

"Why would I trust a drow, sister?" the high elf replied.

"Point taken, but you tried to kill us," Vhaidra retorted.

"It was not me; I was controlled."

"How so? Tell me your whole story."

"Well, apparently, you are *doppelgangers* of our group, but not exactly. For instance, you appear to be lovers with your human cleric. Our human Cleric, Alric, had relations with me, but it was at our undead necromancer, the orc lich Sudagog's wish. Sudagog, being undead, could not be a lover, not having fleshy parts, so he would enter the mind of Alric and be my lover."

"Ick!"

"Ick, indeed. However, he did love me. The feelings were mu... the feelings... I did not consent to this; he controlled me by his necromancy. It is a very powerful magick."

"I'm so sorry to hear that."

"Thank you. Our half-ogre wizard, Blossthus, was the lover of our dwelf, El'ienna."

"I don't know how that is possible; he was so big, and she was so small."

"It was not comfortable to watch. Blossthus was a sadist, and El'ienna was a masochist. Sudagog made us all watch their painful trysts."

"By the Dark Mother!" she blurted out, out of habit.

"I'm not sure how much mind control he had over the others, but we were a force to be reckoned with for years, destroying everything that came in our way, until you five appeared. Anyway, enough about these corpses, how did your group come together and come to be here?"

Vhaidra retold the story of her meeting Hypo outside Sicyon, then Ti'erra, next Elder Dionysios, and finally, how she created Skeletogre. She told them about their relationships, and how they had been brought here by the machinations of the drow priestess, Irriina of House Tekken'duis.

Feyrdryl was shocked. Their stories somewhat matched up. She told Vhaidra how she had been attacked by a group of drow and left for dead when Alric had found her. Alric obviously had feelings for her, but the high elf found him disgusting. She had met El'ienna at a club where she stripped for gold when Alric had taken her there with his *master*, Blossthus. Blossthus and El'ienna were obviously enthralled with one another, and Alric hoped the scene would make Feyrdryl feel in the mood for love. She continued to reject his advances, so Alric went to a powerful lich, Sudagog, and paid him to make her want to have relations with him.

She continued, "Alric did not get exactly what he asked for, but so desiring a beautiful high elf female, he accepted his fate, and was my surrogate lover, which due to mind control, I was able to bear if not exactly enjoy."

"So, I guess you are glad to see them all dead?"

"Yes and no. I am, but in a way, I miss them. They were my constant companions for quite a while now. Plus, as I said, I am pregnant."

"It is Alric's?"

"I am not sure, I mean, it could only be, but perhaps, Sudagog mystically impregnated me too. Either way, my baby is a half-elf and either half-human or half-orc."

"But the Orc, Sudagog, was *undead.* Would the child be undead?"

"I honestly don't know about such things, sister."

"Me neither; we will ask the elder as he appears to be waking now."

Elder Dionysios had been watching the whole thing. Her story was very sad, but he did not know if he could believe her either. But since he now knew for sure that she had an unborn child in her womb, he knew he must protect her and the baby from harm. From his studies, he felt that the child would not be undead, but likely half-human and half-elf, with perhaps innate necromancy skills from Sudagog. Feyrdryl seemed relieved, knowing that her child would be more accepted with this combination.

DAY 198

Vhaidra made food for Feyrdryl, and the great smell woke everyone else, who were soon informed about their new party member. Once they were ready to head out, Dionysios insisted that the high elf ride inside of the ribcage of Skeletogre as she led the way to help them back to where they came from. He told her that this was for her and the baby's protection, which was true, but it also was to ensure none of them ended up with her dual scimitars in their hearts.

CHAPTER XIX
NEW LIFE FROM THE WOMB

Elder Dionysios pulled Skeletogre's cape shut so that the High Elf's nearly naked form would not stir up any passions. She could still see out the front of his ribcage. Feyrdryl did not like being shut-in like this, but she knew following their rules would ensure her survival and thus, the survival of her unborn child.

They travelled until dinnertime, at which time she got out and stretched. She talked about her life when she had joined the team of criminals. Together, they had found adventurers and stole their treasure, while their deaths powered up their master. He did not need to eat, drink, or sleep and only killed. He rarely fought but directed the others how to fight.

El'ienna was the only other drow that Feyrdryl had ever befriended, and she was only half-drow. It was odd to her, but Feyrdryl and Vhaidra got along really well in such a short time; perhaps, because Vhaidra had shown mercy on her and her unborn child. Dionysios was suspicious of how quickly the high elf had befriended Vhaidra the dark elf. He constantly kept an eye on her.

Ti'erra nudged the elder, whispering, "So, Wizard, you seem to like looking at our assassin friend with her skimpy chainmail!"

"No, not at all. I just do not believe she is what she appears to be," he replied gruffly.

"Six months pregnant?" Ti'erra asked.

"No, not that. I just don't think she can be trusted."

"Oh, ok. I won't be jealous then, Wizard," she laughed, skipping away gaily.

"Hmmm, assassin indeed," he mused, ignoring Ti'erra's constant flirtations.

After dinner, the group continued to travel. It was a few hours before they reached their destination, a glowing purple room with a drow priestess in the middle. It was *Priestess Irriina of House Tekken'duis.*

"What? How did you escape your doppelgangers?" she screamed. "No matter. I will destroy you all myself, then I will enter this portal and destroy all of your loved ones too!" she continued, cackling while pointing to a portal she opened with her wand. Vhaidra wondered why this was the third drow female they had found alone, with no entourage. It seemed so odd. But now was not the time for answering that question. The team burst into action, splitting up, Vhaidra throwing her daggers, Dionysios calling for the Uncreated Light, while Nikodemos, Ti'erra, and Skeletogre charged the priestess from different directions.

The dark elf priestess surrounded them in darkness, which only thoroughly blinded Nikodemos and Dionysios, but shortly after she did this, the Uncreated Light came down and *blinded* the priestess.

"Vhaidra, take us into the portal!" the elder instructed since Vhaidra had perfect *dark vision.*

"Time to get out, Feyrdryl! Thank you and goodbye," Vhaidra said, and then did as requested, calling for Skeletogre and the dwelf to follow her. She grabbed her Hypo and the elder, leading them in.

Ti'erra hammered the toes of the priestess, freezing them, and then followed. The priestess blindly threw her five-snake whip out, and it bound Skeletogre with his hands at his side, making him unable to move and making the high elf unable to exit his rib cage. The drow priestess blindly reached out to touch him, to sap his life force. She screamed in anger when she realised it was a skeleton, and then, screamed in pain, as the high elf inside of his rib cage, punctured her heart and lungs with the dual scimitars. Still wrapped up in the five-snake whip and with Feyrdryl's scimitars still stuck in the drow priestess, Skeletogre followed his last command and ran into the portal just before it closed.

"Nooooooooo!" screamed Feyrdryl, clawing at Skeletogre's rib cage.

CHAPTER XX
YOUR WORLD OR MINE?

DAY 298

"Noooooooooo! That was not supposed to happen!" screamed a pained Feyrdryl from inside Skeletogre.

"Us surviving?" asked Elder Dionysios while holding his upset stomach.

Ti'erra violently threw up her last meal, the portal having caused digestive issues beyond what had happened last time.

"Ugh! No...," the high elf replied, "...No. No! I was not supposed to come with you. I was supposed to be left behind, in my own world and in my own time!"

She grabbed her now much larger belly and let go of her scimitars as the five-snake whip released its hold on Skeletogre, and the dead priestess' dead body fell to the ground. Ti'erra crushed the snakes' heads with her greathammer.

"What is your world, and what is our world?" asked Vhaidra.

"I am not sure. Considering that you took portals to and from my world and that your group is a twisted version of mine, I figured they must be different worlds. I can feel the temporal effects of these portals – each time one enters and then exits, one goes forward one hundred days. My baby and womb are much bigger now."

"What if they are not different worlds but simply different parts of the same world?" Elder Dionysios queried.

"That would be much better."

"I believe that to be the case," he explained.

"Oh, good!" the high elf screamed, "Now, how do I go home?"

"Go right for about three-thousand yards and your destination will be on the left," joked Ti'erra, wiping vomit from the corner of her mouth.

"Really?"

"No, I don't know; just a *little dwarven* humour."

Feyrdryl didn't find it funny at all. She looked at the dwelf with disdain. Ti'erra thought she saw hatred. '*Maybe, the wizard was right?*' she thought to herself.

"Very well, you can make your next adventure be *finding Feyrdryl's home!*" she puffed.

Vhaidra pointed out that Feyrdryl should lie down as she looked like she could have her baby any moment now.

"Not so fast!" shouted Dionysios as he pointed to the top of the cliff they were standing below. Up above them were coming a herd of wild animals that had been chased off the cliff.

Everyone ran away and watched as the animals fell to their death, becoming a twisted mess of death. Up above, a group of three *owlbears* stood and watched them before turning and running down the other side of the cliff, which was a steep hill.

"Prepare for battle!" Vhaidra screamed.

"Back away from their prey!" responded the Elder.

All of them heeded his advice and moved back slowly. The owlbears came charging from the backside of the hill cliff, but stopped at their prey, watching the adventurers walk backwards. The monsters began to eat and watched the adventurers as they continued to eat.

"No need to fight if we can avoid it," the elder explained.

"Coward!" shouted Feyrdryl.

"Shush, Assassin!" sharply replied Ti'erra, "The wizard is far wiser than you!" Being called an assassin quieted the high elf completely, "Great strategy, Wizard!"

"Thank you, Ti'erra."

The group found bushes to sit behind and prepared their supper. From there, they could see the now far away owlbears eating their intended prey along with the footless corpse of the dead drow priestess and the snakes from her whip. Feyrdryl came out of

Skeletogre's ribcage to eat with the other adventurers. She began warily talking to the cleric while the other party members spoke among themselves.

"What a horrible fate for the body of a priestess!" Vhaidra sighed.

"Serves her right!" remarked Ti'erra.

"Vhaidra is right, it would be better if we could bury her body, rather than let it be eaten by wild beasts," the elder explained.

"We can still bury her when they are done, can we not, Wizard?"

"Yes, but one should be buried whole, if possible."

"Monk, wouldn't she be a powerful skeleton to raise?"

"Yes, possibly, but also dangerous," Vhaidra replied.

"I guess so," Ti'erra conceded.

"Ladies, let's be sure to have two on every watch again tonight. I still don't trust that high elf," Dionysios whispered.

"But she saved us, Elder!"

"I am not entirely convinced that was intentional," he replied. "Vhaidra, please watch her while we do evening prayers tonight."

"Okay," she sighed and went to talk to Feyrdryl, who had just finished chatting with Hypo. He then left her to talk to the elder.

"Your Hypo is much kinder than my Alric was, sister. You are lucky to have him."

"I am so sorry you were abused in such a way by your teammates. Thankfully your time of suffering is over."

"Yeah, I guess."

"So, Feyrdryl, what are your plans for your child? Will you raise it on your own or give it up to an orphanage?"

"I honestly do not know. He or she will not look like a high elf for sure. I am already rare, having jet-black hair, but his or her father having dark-brown skin and being human, he or she may look more like a wood elf than a high elf!"

"Will your fellow high elves accept such a child?"

"Unfortunately, no. Should I keep him or her, it will have to be away from my fellow high elves."

"Perhaps with the wood elves?"

"Mayhap."

With that, she got up and wandered away in meditation. Vhaidra joined her to comfort her new friend while the others did evening prayers before rest.

"Would your drow accept a mixed child if you and your Hypo mated, sister?" Feyrdryl asked.

"Only as a slave. The only acceptable half-drow are *half-demons* and dryders."

"So, you may have to face a similar decision as mine?"

"I do not expect Hypo to die if I allow him to breed me," she explained.

"I did not plan those deaths either!" the high elf sharply stated, anger and hatred flashing in her eyes.

"Sorry, I didn't mean..."

"It's ok. Let's get our elven reverie, sister."

"Good plan."

The two elves went into reverie and awoke with Elder Dionysios and Ti'erra standing watch over them.

DAY 299

"Good morning! We can take it from here, you two." Feyrdryl said, stifling a yawn.

"Vhaidra, raise Skeletogre before we rest, please."

Vhaidra raised the crumbled Skeletogre, and the two elves watched the fire and talked as Skeletogre marched around their camp and the others rested.

CHAPTER XXI
DEN OF MURDERERS

In the morning, after morning prayers and break-fast, the team tried to find some sign of how to find a city to buy supplies. They had no idea where they were, other than a desert near some isolated mountains and a bunch of bushes near the mountains.

After wandering for a while, they finally found a cave in one of the mountains and entered it. In no time at all, they realised that they were in a labyrinth.

"A labyrinth in the desert...," Elder Dionysios noted, "This may be the den of a *copper dragon*. Thankfully, they are good dragons and do not like to fight."

"That is good," Feyrdryl looked down at the ground. The Cleric Alric and El'ienna had made armour from the skin of an old copper dragon that their team had killed, even though the dragon wanted nothing to do with fighting them. In the fight, she had got hurt and almost died. The cone of *slow gas* that the dragon breathed made it impossible for her to defend herself or attack in time to be really useful.

Ti'erra suddenly felt ashamed of the under armour that she was wearing. She wondered if the copper dragons could smell the hide she was wearing.

She would not have to wonder for long.

Suddenly, there was a gust of wind as two copper dragons flew around them.

"So, we have murderers of old copper dragons in our midst, eh? While we copper dragons are generally peaceful, you will find that when you kill our family members, that we can be extremely brutal," the male dragon raged.

Before anyone could do anything, both dragons breathed slow gas on them, slowing all of their movements, save for Skeletogre, to a crawl.

Elder Dionysios knew it would take a lot of time, but a *teleport chant* was the only way to get everyone out alive. Vhaidra started to start to chant a darkness spell. The dragons spit acid towards Skeletogre. Skeletogre dodged the attack, but the acid still hit Feyrdryl's chainmail armour, eroding it all away.

Ti'erra handed her hammer to the undead ogre and slowly shouted, "*Tttbhh... rrrr... ooo... www... iii... ttt!*"

Skeletogre understood, spun around the greathammer by its leather loop, and launched it at one of the two dragons, hitting it directly in its jaw, knocking it out, and freezing its head. Ti'erra then very slowly took off her dragon scale armour bikini from under her suede leather tunic dress and handed it to Feyrdryl, so that she would not be naked, for the sake of the wizard and the monk's cleric.

The remaining dragon spit another attack at Skeletogre, and he avoided it hitting his bones again, with it hitting Feyrdryl's dragon scale armour that she had barely placed on her body. Thankfully, the armour was acid-resistant, and it did not dissolve like her mail armour. Ti'erra shouted out to Skeletogre, "*Ggg... eee... ttt... tttbhh... eee... hhh... aaa... mmmmmm... eeerrr!*"

Skeletogre obtained the greathammer he had thrown and was getting ready to launch it again when the whole room went pitch-black. Then, there was a flash of blue light, and they all, including the copper dragon, were teleported outside to the other side of the mountain from where they started. When they teleported, the slow gas remained in the cave, so within moments, everyone was back at full speed.

The metallic dragon was very confused. Nikodemos launched his newly-obtained enchanted solid jade Yan Yue Dao like a spear, Vhaidra threw six daggers, and Skeletogre launched Ti'erra's greathammer at the copper dragon. The cleric's Yan Yue Dao pierced the dragon's throat while the daggers spread to pierce its wings, and the hammer broke the flying creature's breastbone, making it fall to the ground.

Feyrdryl had crawled from Skeletogre and tossed the undead creature's dual scimitars to Ti'erra, shouting to her to follow her. The two women ran while in a squatting position towards the dragon. After the high elf had shown where they should hit, they jabbed the four scimitars into pressure points that took the beast close to death. Unfortunately,

Feyrdryl's scimitars went deep into the dragon, even the handles going below the skin! Nikodemos' concurrent twisting and pulling off his Yan Yue Dao was enough to be the final blow that killed the dragon, even though the acid from the enchanted jade had no effect on the beast.

Feyrdryl started to dig for her scimitars, but the elder shouted out, "We don't have time for that. I can now see a town ahead. Let's head there immediately!" She argued that they had all the time in the world, but the elder mentioned that the other dragon would awake and find her dead mate soon enough, and there was no reason to fight a copper dragon if it was not absolutely necessary.

Feyrdryl was fuming, but crawled back into Skeletogre, this time of her own desire, and headed to the town ahead. She would just have to trade in the copper dragon scale armour for some new weapons and some armour that would not have dragons hunting her for. She would have liked to have bought plate mail armour, but out of respect for her dark elf sister, she would get something without metal, as the other adventurers had apparently done.

CHAPTER XXII
SHOP UNTIL YOU DIE

Once the adventurers had arrived in the seaside city, the high elf was able to trade the copper dragon scale armour to a wood elf trader for a sylvan ranger's *bow and arrows*, along with a full set of proper leather armour and a long fire-coloured proper *fey dress*. She told Vhaidra that in her youth, she had been very good with a bow and arrow, but she would rather have been able to trade for dual scimitars, which she had been using for a long time. Unfortunately, she could not find any twin scimitars of suitable quality.

Vhaidra was very happy to see her new friend switch to a ranged weapon and leather armour. This meant she would not have to worry about rust monsters attacking them, due to her metal armour and weapons. It also gave them a ranged unit in combat. They could always use more since none of her other teammates were really set up for multiple ranged attacks.

The elder was also glad for the weapon and armour change. Her clothing was not in any way modest before, nor did it do any good protecting her. Plus, he had less reason to fear his life ending due to scimitars in his back. The elder and the hypodiakonos found the local episkopos and gave ten per cent of their treasure to him. *Episkopos Andrew* was shocked, as he knew neither man nor their episkopos. "You are very far from your Sicyon if it is near Corinth. You are in *Rakote*, on the other side of the sea. It must be at least six hundred miles away from Corinth by ship. How did you get here?"

The two men explained to Episkopos Andrew, who took notes and then offered for them to pray together. He gave Nikodemos a new white robe, a black vest, and a black skufiya hat to wear over his red dragon scale armour so that he appeared as a proper hypodiakonos. The designs of the robe, vest, and skufiya hat were a little different here in the state of *Misr*, as compared to *Hellas*, but he still liked them. Afterwards, they left, and the elder bought *true seeing ointment* for two hundred fifty gold pieces before they met the rest of the group at the *Sanstefano Inn* in which they stayed.

Vhaidra was impressed to see her Hypo in new, clean robes again. It had been quite a while since she had shaved him, and his beard had been coming back quickly. It had grown much more quickly than his hair on the top of his head. She decided that she could live with his beard after all. Moreover, it was not knotted in dreadlocks like the elder's and was instead, kept clean, brushed, and neat.

That night, two things happened. First, the surviving copper dragon flew into town and destroyed the family of the trader who had bought the copper dragon scale armour with his *acid breath* attack. Secondly, Ti'erra could have sworn that during her elven reverie, that Feyrdryl claimed to truly be an *obsidian dragon* and not truly pregnant at all.

DAY 300

In the morning, the elder chanted to make a *zone of truth*, then put the true seeing ointment in his eyes, and began to interrogate the high elf in the shared ladies' room, with Skeletogre and Nikodemos present, in addition to the ladies in residence.

The questions he asked were not directly talking about her and her past, but he was able to keep her off guard with the odd questions and saw the truth. What he saw, not only scared him but shocked him to his core. He could not believe that this was even possible!

"Your unborn baby is not a half-elf!" he exclaimed.

"Then, what is her baby, Wizard?" asked Ti'erra.

"It is a half-dragon; it is a half obsidian dragon!"

"WHAT!" everyone gasped.

Feyrdryl tried to explain. She told them that Sudagog's master was an obsidian dragon.

"So, you were offered as a pet to the obsidian dragon too?" Vhaidra asked.

Feyrdryl lowered her head in shame, unable to answer.

Ti'erra asked, "What will it look like, Wizard?"

"Well Ti'erra, the baby will look like a human, but anywhere a human male would have hair, this child will have grey scales that eventually will turn shiny black and be razor-sharp. In time, it may grow horns as well."

"The assassin is going to have an interesting baby!" Ti'erra replied excitedly.

"Yes, but that does not explain why the child is not a half-elf!" the elder added.

"Was it because of magickal manipulation?" the high elf asked quite innocently, looking around.

Dionysios began, "One could say that, but you know and I now also know that it is because you are not *fey*, but instead you are truly a wy...," but before he could finish, Feyrdryl swiftly grabbed Skeletogre's dual scimitars and struck the elder with both of them. Before she could turn around after attacking him, her neck was sliced open by a poisoned dagger. Gurgling noises came from the high elf's open throat as she fixated her eyes on her attacker, dropping the twin scimitars. The elder cried out in pain, but then instructed Nikodemos, "Make haste! Cut the baby out of the womb NOW, before she dies!"

"You may have called me sister, but nobody tries to kill my friends, or they get killed first!" Vhaidra replied, looking closely at the high elf, who had a hopeless look in her eyes. Nikodemos was confused but did what he was told by the elder as Vhaidra was twisting Feyrdryl's neck. The hypodiakonos cut a c-shape at the bottom of her belly, pulled the baby out, and cut its umbilical cord just as Vhaidra twisted the high elf's neck three hundred sixty degrees, breaking her neck, and kissed her cheek, whispering, "Goodbye and good death, 'sister.'" As soon as the neck snapped, Feyrdryl's body morphed...

...into the form of a dead obsidian dragon! The size increase of her form destroyed the room, spilling them all out onto the ground.

The innkeeper ran out to see what happened. Ti'erra lied and said that the obsidian dragon had come looking for him, the innkeeper, so they had killed it. Seeing the baby that was crying, he said, "Oh, thank you! Your pregnant party member had her baby?"

Ti'erra looked to the ground, and cried, picking up the dress that Feyrdryl had worn, "Yes, but the obsidian dragon killed her as she gave birth!" The innkeeper was apologetic, wanting to pay them for their loss, but Nikodemos told him that they would not take funds from him, and since they were unable to protect his inn, they would pay him. The innkeeper refused, and Vhaidra suggested that he simply take the hide from the dragon, which would give him enough profit for fixing the inn and expanding it. The innkeeper said that they should take it, as it was his fault that they had lost a party member, and now, looking at the elder, he realised he was hurt. Again, Nikodemos refused, so the innkeeper called on his personal apothecary to help the cleric heal his friend and to find a *milkmaid* to feed the baby.

Although he was healed as much as possible within the hour, Dionysios found that he could not move his arms due to nerve damage from the twin strikes to biceps. His hands were balled into fists. So, Nikodemos put his Budding Staff in his hands, where he held it well.

Episkopos Andrew of Rakote arrived. He was not happy. "Within twelve hours of your arrival, this city has had two dragon attacks. I think for the good of these people, you should leave," he scolded them, "Furthermore, I do not give you a blessing to stay any longer; I only give you a blessing to leave." The episkopos had already decided to write a letter to their episkopos and ban them from ever entering Rakote ever again.

The elder and hypodiakonos took the blessing to leave, and Dionysios began to chant. Again, four *warhorses* arrived. Nikodemos helped the elder get on the white horse, tying the staff to it, so he would not fall; he helped Vhaidra onto the black horse, giving her a kiss. Nikodemos was surprised to see Skeletogre on the yellow horse, so he helped Ti'erra, who was holding the baby, onto the red horse.

He walked back over to Vhaidra and asked, "Permission to board, mistress?" in jest. Vhaidra smiled and affirmed his request. Once ready, they took off at astronomical speeds. "Where to, Elder?" the hypodiakonos asked.

"We're going back home. Our mission is complete!"

Nikodemos was confused and wary, but while Vhaidra held him tight, he continued chanting for the healing of his elder. Ti'erra was scared. They were going back to the home of the Jet Fist Cult, who had been seeking to kill them. But she also was very curious. "What are we going to call the baby, and how will we feed him?"

"His name is Mikhail," the elder stated matter-of-the-factly. He continued, "We will stop in every town and hire a milkmaid until we get home. Hold him tight!"

The dwelf did as she was told, cooing at the baby and feeling maternal pangs.

CHAPTER XXIII
HOMEWARD BOUND

"So, why did we have to cut the baby out before Feyrdryl reverted to her obsidian dragon form?" Nikodemos asked.

"Dragons do not have wombs. They lay eggs. In high elf form, she had a womb, but there is no saying what might have happened to Mikhail when she changed form. He may have ended up in her bowels and died."

"Wow, why did you suspect her, Elder?"

"I sensed evil from her immediately, and then when she shared her stories, I heard deceit. When she looked around, I saw hidden hate in her eyes. Ti'erra saw this hatred once too, I believe."

"I did, Wizard!"

"It took me a while, and I wasn't sure what the reason was. So, not wanting to judge her unfairly, I put her to the test. Being a dragon, she arrogantly thought she could pass without a problem. She was wrong."

"Why did you save her baby, Elder? Won't it be evil, being half obsidian dragon?" Vhaidra asked.

"No one is born evil, not even dark elves," chuckled Dionysios. "You were raised to be evil, Vhaidra, and you were able to remove this from yourself and become friends with many overworlders and even learned to love. I think Mikhail has the right to live and should not be held liable for his parents' sins. In fact, I believe that the Armour sent us on this very adventure to save Mikhail and to take him to the Orphanage of the Transfiguration Cenobium. It is the very reason that we were brought together."

"So, we will go our separate ways once we return to Sicyon?" whimpered Ti'erra.

Everyone was surprised by the elder's answer. "May it not be so! What therefore The Ancient of Days hath joined together, let not man put asunder."

"Yippee!" squealed the dwelf, reaching over and squeezing the elder's arm.

"I thought you preferred being a hermit, Elder?" Nikodemos queried.

"This is true, but now I have an affinity for this group, and I believe that The Ancient of Days has brought us together with a purpose, possibly beyond our first mission to save Mikhail."

Vhaidra squeezed her Hypo tighter with a big smile on her face. Her weak prayers secretly taught to her by the elder at night had been answered. "Thank you, Most Holy Theotokos!" she inaudibly whispered.

As planned, they stopped at each town, hired a milkmaid to feed Mikhail, and changed his swaddling clothes. They did not take time to visit the episkopos of each town, but rather only took time to hire a milkmaid for Mikhail, eat, and move on.

DAY 301

When they got to *Halab,* one day later, the elder instructed them to stop. "The horses will stop here. We will hire a milkmaid to journey with us now. We will join a caravan to the sea, where we will ride on a ship to our destination."

"Why, Wizard?" Ti'erra asked.

"It is not auspicious to continue by horse," he replied, this time allowing everyone to get off the horses before they faded away.

That night, having regained the full use of his lower arms, the elder found a monastic orphanage so that he could inquire about hiring any available milkmaids for the rest of their trip. He found one of their faith, and paid her family half of her salary first, promising her the rest when they arrived at their home. Her name was *Miriam.* She had long, dark-brown hair and skin that was darker than Ti'erra's. She had lost her child in birth and had since then dedicated her life to giving babies the life-giving nutrition that only a mother's breasts could give. She volunteered at the *Theophany Orphanage* every day, giving babies milk from newborns to toddlers. Other mothers did the same daily volunteer work, so the orphanage was fine with Miriam going on the journey. "Why don't you just leave this baby with Theophany Orphanage?" Miriam asked.

"I would. However, I believe that he is destined to follow the same path as I at the same orphanage where I was raised."

"I understand, Elder."

The elder and Miriam returned to the *Merchant Inn,* where she was introduced to everyone. The elder rented a room for Miriam and the baby. Ti'erra volunteered to stay with them for the night. Vhaidra had planned to room with Ti'erra, as usual, save for when she was learning new spells but agreed to this change of plans and to bunk alone.

Miriam noticed the scales on Mikhail's body and asked Ti'erra to run to the apothecary for *calendula cream,* which would soften the baby's skin. Ti'erra gave Miriam Feyrdryl's bow and arrows to hold, in case she needed to protect herself.

During the night, when Mikhail cried in the adjacent room, Nikodemos woke up and asked what was happening, seeing the Eeder and Vhaidra sitting near each other on Dionysios' bed. That night, while Nikodemos slept, the elder did as he had been doing secretly every night, *catechising* Vhaidra about The Way. When staying in an inn, they did this in the room that the elder and hypodiakonos shared, so no one would ever get the wrong idea. Thankfully, the hypodiakonos was unaware, as he was a sound sleeper.

Vhaidra explained that she wanted to learn more about The Way, but that she preferred to learn it from someone other than her beloved Hypo. She felt she was more open to question the faith when being taught by the elder. Also, he was more patient and less judgemental. Nikodemos had to agree but wished they had not kept it secret from him.

Mikhail stopped crying quickly, being satiated by Miriam's breast.

"Had you known, Nikodemos, you would have pushed her too hard, and she would not have considered a conversion. In fact, you may have lost her. Be patient and let her learn from me, and perhaps, one day, she can be your wife."

Vhaidra immediately raised the question of why they had to marry one of The Way. This had initially come up when they had first met the elder. The drow monk had bit her tongue on this issue until now.

"We believe," the elder began, "that when a couple marries, they become *one flesh,* and one flesh can only worship one God. The Ancient of Days cannot bless a marriage where say, for instance, the Spider Queen is worshipped by this One flesh."

"I guess that makes sense, but why are your couples not intimate before marriage?"

Nikodemos' face flushed as he happily listened to the elder answer Vhaidra's questions, now glad that he was not answering the questions after all.

"It is the same reason. One can only become one flesh with one that one has dedicated their own life with. One cannot unite one's flesh with many others, or they lose themselves and become polluted."

"I think I understand. I never mated, because I was a monk in a monastery from my youth, but most female drow will take whatever male they desire until they no longer want him, then discard him like a pet or a favourite dish."

"Virginity is very valued in both our society and religion," the elder continued, "If you and Nikodemos are both virgins and marry, you are giving one another a very special gift."

"I guess I never thought of it that way. I will have to think this over. Thank you for the lesson, Elder," she kissed her Hypo and left to her room.

"Thank you, Elder. I do hope that one day that I will have her accept to be my wife if it is to be the Will of the Creator-Logos-Ghost."

"It will take time. Be patient. Her catechesis may take longer, due to her coming from the Spider Queen's society that worshipped an evil demon queen as a Goddess. She does adore the Theotokos, but worshipping The Ancient of Days may take more time. Our example, as followers of The Way, is the best thing to help her convert."

"I understand, Elder. Thank you again and goodnight."

"May The Ancient of Days grant it," Dionysios replied.

Nikodemos grabbed his icon, kissed it, and said a prayer to the mother of his God.

DAY 302

In the morning, after morning prayers and their breakfast, they joined the caravan to the sea. The caravan trip was uneventful, but the travel by sea was anything but!

CHAPTER XXIV
AGED LIKE FINE WINE

It was not long after their journey by ship began that Elder Dionysios regained use of his hands. It was just in time too, as a group of pirates pulled up next to the ship. These pirates had an ingenious way of taking over a ship. They had a wizard who used an *ageing* spell that aged everyone on the ship by twenty years. Captains of a ship were often sixty and many of the crew and passengers were in their forties and older. So, they aged to an age where they were not much trouble when the pirates ransacked the ship, or sometimes aged to death!

So, as was their *modus operandi*, they started putting out boarding planks. Many of the crew, anticipating what would happen next, actually abandoned the ship!

The passengers, completely unaware, were all aged twenty years older. This made the elder very old and frail. This should have made Nikodemos fifty-three years old, but for some reason, he did not appear to age, but his black hair reached the ground behind him, and his beard grew to belly length in front of him. Vhaidra and Ti'erra aged, but twenty years was so little that one could not tell that they aged, especially Vhaidra, who, as a monk, was even slower to show age than a normal drow!

Elder Dionysios started to chant a *cure* chant. He only had the strength to maybe, cure himself, and he did not know how long he could continue chanting in his aged and weakened state. After he was cured, he would cure the others, if possible.

The milkmaid, Miriam, sat down to feed Mikhail when suddenly he grew to twenty years old sitting on her lap. Mikhail understood nothing except what his half-human/half-dragon nature told him. That nature was telling him that the men on the other boat were going to hurt the people who loved him and the others on his boat.

His nature told him to open his mouth and breathe fire on them, and then they would go away. The pirates never knew what hit them. They had never expected that a half-dragon baby would be on board. It ended up being their final mistake as they burned to death along with their vessel.

The elder felt his death approaching him imminently and finished his chant just in time to roll back his age twenty years. Thanking The Ancient of Days, he began to chant to de-age the others.

Miriam was in shock, "Elder Dionysios, you are right. This is a very special boy. I do hope the mothers at your orphanage can help him control his powers. Today, this newborn killed twenty men and is totally unaware." She had been unaware that Mikhail was half-dragon, nor did she realise that this was ever possible.

"I believe he will not have this power again until he ages to adulthood, but you are right. He must learn when and where to use his powers, as he has been blessed with special powers by his very birth."

"Amin."

Vhaidra and Ti'erra walked up to the Elder to check on him, and then complained about them not being de-aged.

"I am sorry, ladies, I do not know a cure spell that would work to de-age elves or dwarves. But it does not look like either of you aged at all."

"Thank you, Wizard, but I will die twenty years earlier now, due to this attack," Ti'erra sadly stated.

"Ti'erra, tomorrow is not promised, let alone twenty years. Do not worry about twenty years, worry about saving your soul today, for today may be your last."

"Fearful words, Wizard."

"Real words of truth," he responded to the dwelf. "Look at those pirates; their last act was an act of evil. Where do their souls belong? Let us not do evil, especially in our unknown last moments."

Elder Dionysios was glad that Mikhail was not a half-elf, as he would not have been able to de-age him, and a twenty-year-old that had only the abilities of a baby would be impossible to deal with, even with the patience of the elder.

Nikodemos checked on Vhaidra. She was crying. "Why are you crying, dear?"

"This is the truth of our relationship. In twenty years' time, I will not physically age, but you will be getting old. You will die, and I will not be old. I will live on for hundreds of more years."

"I plan on living forever, Vhaidra!" he smirked. "Did you not see, my hair only grew, and I did not feel any older at all!"

The old Vhaidra would have hit him hard, but instead, she just hugged him, not sure if he was right, still crying and saying, "I love you, Hypo. Don't ever leave me!"

"I never will, dear. I love you too."

The couple kissed. Ti'erra sighed. Dionysios rested. Miriam fed Mikhail. Mikhail pooped in his swaddling clothes. Meanwhile, the Captain yelled at the crew members who had abandoned ship, hitting them with oars as they floated in the water and ordering them to come back on board. After he finally received the abandoning crew, he came back and thanked the elder, telling him that he and his friends could sleep in the Captain's Den, two at a time, as long as the rest of them kept watch for more invading pirate ships. Miriam was most grateful to go rest with Mikhail on the first shift of sleep. Unfortunately, for the passengers on the ship, this was not the last time they would be attacked, although at least no more pirates bothered them on their voyage.

CHAPTER XXV
DEAD URCHINS

DAY 303

Elder Dionysios finally had full use of his fingers again. It took a while, but the various healing potions and chants had healed him very well, having started at his shoulders and working their way down to his fingertips.

Before they got to their first stop at *Rodos,* they came upon an old skeleton of a ship that appeared abandoned. It was interesting, but soon, they forgot about it, as their own ship was surrounded by *sharks* and attacked by a dozen *zombies* who had died by drowning in the sea.

The beings were fast and furious and attacked the crew first. The *Captain* and his *first mate* were among the first to die. Miriam and Ti'erra were sleeping in the *Captain's Deck* and hearing the ruckus, they ran up to see what was happening, leaving the sleeping Mikhail on the bed below.

Elder Dionysios signalled to Nikodemos and started chanting to call down the Uncreated Light, knowing this would destroy the undead creatures. Vhaidra decided not to waste time by calling her acid cloud; instead, she did what she loved most, using her fists and feet to destroy these sea-drowned zombies.

Following the signal that he received from the elder, Nikodemos caught the zombies at the base of their spines with his Yan Yue Dao and flung them over the ship, into the water. Due to the acid damage from the mystical jade weapon, they broke in half upon hitting the water. Ti'erra used her greathammer to crush the monsters. Even though Miriam still had Feyrdryl's bow and arrows that Ti'erra had given her, she ran back down to watch Mikhail, having her weapon ready only if the creatures advanced towards her position. Skeletogre was skirmishing with two of the sea-drowned zombies and found his scimitars very successful against them.

By the time each of the adventurers, save for Dionysios, had killed, maimed, or broken two of the creatures, their apparent boss hopped aboard, an evil *seacat*!

Just then, the Uncreated Light came down from the heavens and destroyed the remaining sea-drowned zombies, and annoyed the seacat, who was blinded by the attack. The seacat swung its claws wildly, destroying the door that led to the Captain's Deck.

But on the other side of the boat appeared a *sahuagin*, a fish-like merman, who was the actual boss of the attacking crew. The seacat was seemingly just its battle animal.

From below, Miriam fired arrow after arrow in rapid succession at the animal's face, making it scream in pain. Vhaidra began throwing daggers at each creature. Nikodemos ran for the seacat and Ti'erra headed for the sahuagin, but she was too late. The creature had already swung its *trident* at Dionysios, who, while able to block the attack with his Budding Staff, flew into the sea. He again began to chant as a shark swam towards him. Skeletogre swung his scimitars towards the sahuagin too but found that the creature was able to block the attack and use the inertia of the attack to knock the mighty undead ogre into the sea as well. Another shark headed towards him.

Nikodemos had more luck, using his Yan Yue Dao to cut the tail off of the Seacat, causing it to spin around from the entrance to the Captain's Deck, which also allowed Miriam to fire the rest of the quiver of arrows into the seacat's bloody backside.

The sahuagin was now having his own troubles as well. Ti'erra had smashed his left hand and trident with her greathammer and swung back as she was about to follow through on his right side.

Vhaidra threw her daggers at the sahuagin, and the hammer strike of her dwelf friend implanted them far into his organs, crushing his right arm and rib cage. He ran over to his seacat and jumped on top of him, ordering him to leave the battle.

Unfortunately for him, seacats were known for fighting to the death, and even its immense pain would not cause the monster to retreat.

While swimming, Dionysios hit the shark close to him with his Budding Staff, causing it to circle back. Skeletogre, also now in the sea, used his scimitars against another shark as he began to sink. After chanting to walk on water, the elder grabbed

Skeletogre's arm and pulled him up on the water's surface, allowing him to walk on water as long as they were in physical contact with one another. The water around them acted like a solid sheet of ice, preventing the sharks' attacks. They walked up to the ship, and Skeletogre climbed up and engaged the seacat again.

The seacat swung wildly again and knocked Nikodemos into the sea as well. The elder ran over the sea to help him up and walked with him back to the ship again. Meanwhile, Ti'erra ran and jumped, implanting her greathammer in the skull of the sahuagin, knocking it completely unconscious and giving it severe brain damage. She then jumped atop the seacat so that she could crush its skull.

Vhaidra carefully aimed and threw three daggers into each eye of the seacat and blinded it. Skeletogre sliced deep cuts into its front paws. The seacat rolled onto its back, knowing that there was a stranger on top of it. Once it did, Ti'erra went flying into the sea and Skeletogre and Vhaidra each targeted its now exposed belly and its vital organs, which allowed them to deliver the final blows. Vhaidra then collected her daggers and Miriam's arrows from the creatures and extracted their teeth and claws for selling. They also took the sahuagin's eyes for eating, unaware that the sahuagin was still alive, but out cold.

Ti'erra used her greathammer to pull herself back up into the ship after the Elder had saved her from drowning, and then, threw a rope down for the two men to pull themselves back up. They all worked together to roll the giant seacat into the sea. As it splashed, they heard the other creature on the ship start to scream in pain, apparently awoken. Nikodemos ran over, and seeing its plight, which he, unfortunately, knew all too well, mercifully stabbed it through the heart, killing it. He then got help to roll it into the sea as well.

The sharks, although pets of the sahuagin just like the seacat, ate both monsters in a bloody feast. Not much of the crew remained, so they knew that once they got to Rodos, they would need to hire another ship. Ti'erra went down to the Captain's Deck and took treasure equivalent to half of their fare so that funds would not be an issue.

When they arrived in Rodos, they were in for quite a surprise.

CHAPTER XXVI

TIME IS THE FIRE IN WHICH WE BURN

Rodos was completely ablaze. There were a *fire giant* and twelve *fire archons* marching through the city. Because of this, the remaining crew decided to avoid the entire island and head towards *Patmos* instead.

Hypodiakonos Nikodemos thought they should try to save the city. The elder pointed out that they would be useless in such a battle, and would not be able to save anyone, not even themselves. Vhaidra was proud of his bravery and selflessness but also agreed with Elder Dionysios.

While the beasts did try to throw some fireballs towards the ship, Ti'erra hit them back towards the city with her enchanted aquamarine encrusted greathammer each time they got close to hitting the ship. Although the enchanted aquamarines installed in her hammer had created a freezing attack, which allowed her to do this, the fireballs, unfortunately, singed her hair.

With the number of deaths on the ship, even with their new destination, their food supplies would thankfully be enough for everyone who had survived when supplemented with fish and seafood they could catch with their nets. The Captain and crew members that had died, along with the deceased passengers were given a proper burial at sea that evening, with the elder and hypodiakonos doing *Trisagion* prayers for the reposed. They would have buried them at Rodos, but that was impossible now, and the risk of sickness was too great to keep them on the ship all the way to Patmos.

DAY 304

The next day was uneventful. It was something that the group needed after back-to-back craziness. During the day, the group chatted among themselves along with the remaining crew and passengers. The passengers were mostly thankful for the adventurers saving them from the many attacks, but some thought that perhaps they were being targeted due to the adventurers being on board and started to complain to the remaining crew. The elder again suggested that at Patmos, they definitely needed to get on a new boat.

While visiting Patmos, he was sure they could stay in monastic cells at the *Monastery of Agiou Ioanni Theologou* in exchange for a small donation that he would provide. It would also allow them to attend the *divine services* of The Way.

When they arrived at Patmos, as planned, they stayed at the monastery. Each had a cell of their own, except for Skeletogre, who stayed in his cape-bag in Elder Dionysios' cell.

DAY 305

The next day, they saw that the ship they had arrived on had left. The dockhand said that they left early in the morning in hopes that the adventurers would not board. The group laughed, seeing that they never planned to ride on that now captain-less boat anyway. They asked the dockhand when the next boat would depart for Corinth. The news was not what they had expected. It was going to be about fifty more days before another ship came that would head that way. Elder Dionysios and Hypodiakonos Nikodemos were excited to get to attend the full cycle of services each day, living in the monastery, and truth be told, Vhaidra was excited to be living in a monastery again and learning more about the faith known as The Way. Ti'erra was fine with staying there, although she liked to go to the local pubs and go shopping during the day, rather than going to all of the many services. Miriam was a pious lady and enjoyed her time in prayer when she did not have to take care of Mikhail. Nikodemos also appreciated the downtime which would give him time to really get to know Vhaidra's soul, as the Dark Dancer had instructed him to do.

DAY 308

This was Mikhail's eighth day, so as was their religion's tradition, Mikhail was officially given his name and made a *katichoumenos* by the episkopos at the monastery. This was the first step to becoming a member of The Way.

DAY 333

Vhaidra figured it was time. She asked Hypo to spend the day with her. They sat in a cave on the beach and talked. She started off by asking how he was able to speak one of her languages to her the first day they met.

"I'm surprised you hadn't asked earlier," he admitted.

"I wanted to figure it out on my own, but I couldn't, so I had to ask," she admitted, frowning.

"Well, long ago, when I was at *Ekpaideftirio*, my clerical school, I studied all the world religions. It is actually how I ended up with my first Yan Yue Dao. I travelled to the Far East to the land of Zhong, where I learned about the local religion of *San Jiao He Yi*. Learning it, I learned how I could lead others to The Way from their understanding of the God that they call *Shang Di*, which I believe to be just a corrupted view of The Ancient of Days."

"But what of the common underworld language?"

"Well, after I learned the human, fey, dwarven, orcish, draconic and other religions of beings in the surface, I learned of the religions of the underworld. While most of them were quite frightening, save for the Dark Dancer, I found myself with an affinity and interest in the good dark elves. I studied the underworld language so that I could not only read translations and third-party observations but could really get to know the religions of the underworld. Studying the language let me learn all of the underworld religions. While learning proper drow language, even though it is really just a dialect of proper elvish, it would have only taught me about the Spider Queen's worship. Learning these other heretical religions actually strengthened my belief in The Way."

"By the Dark M... that is fascinating, Hypo!"

"You think so?"

"Yes, because I did almost the same thing. In the monasteries, I learned a little about overworld religions. But I never knew about the various religions of the underworld, other than worshipping the Spider Queen. Admitting they existed would have given those Goddesses power, I guess. But in learning of the kindness of many of the overworld Goddesses, and how they loved their worshippers, unlike the Dark Mother who used her worshippers as pawns, I found myself rejecting the Goddess. It had the opposite effect on my sistren, as they found the overworld Goddesses as weak with even weaker followers. So, I had to keep my feelings to myself and worked on removing all of the Spider Queen's vestiges from my mind, body, and soul.

As such, I worked harder at my bright light training, so that, perhaps, one day, the Gods of the overworld would allow me to come out of the underworld and feel their love personally, if it really existed, and was not just stuff of fairytales, which I feared."

"*Agape*: the love to and from The Ancient of Days is just as real as *eros*: love of beauty, *philia*: love of friends, *storge*: love of children and parents, and *xenia*: love of foreigners and guests. We share that love in the meals after our divine services. I believe that everything happens for a reason. Everything is an opportunity given to us from the Creator-Logos-Ghost. Look at all of the bad things that happened to you that caused you to come to the overworld and learn of the love of The Ancient of Days."

"Perhaps, it is something to consider. Thank you, Hypo," Vhaidra said and then got up, held her Hypo's hand, and walked down the beach with him.

DAY 339

On his fortieth day, Mikhail would receive the *mysteries* of *vaptisma* (ritualistic washing in holy water), *chrisma* (ritualistic anointing with holy oil), *koura* (offering the first sacrifice of hair), and his first *koinonia* for (an unknown mystery to all except full members of The Way) to become a full member of their faith. The elder would be his *nounos* (sponsor) in entering into The Way. Until that day, Mikhail had stayed in the back of the monastery's temple with Vhaidra and Ti'erra. Only full initiates were allowed in the front of the temple. Watching these mysteries, Vhaidra made the decision to convert to the faith of her Hypo and secretly, said this to the elder.

DAY 345

After being on the island for forty days, Ti'erra had gained enough intelligence from gossiping drunks at the pubs to report that the Jet Fist Cult had grown in size and power in Sicyon. Zyx'Vuts, its five feet and ten inches tall elven leader and an acolyte of five different evil deities, had made Sicyon his new home and was promising to bring the evil God, Lord Kajne, to the city soon. This would not be a happy homecoming.

DAY 346

On his forty-eighth day, Mikhail had his chrisma washed off. After the services this day, Vhaidra insisted that they battle plan for their return to Sicyon. After they came up with their plan, she raised Skeletogre, and they practised their battle plans. They agreed to do this daily until their boat arrived. Once raised, the monks at the monastery banned Skeletogre from staying at the monastery. So, they had him stand guard at the abandoned docks each night instead.

DAY 350

Skeletogre killed five *kobolds* who arrived on a boat, wearing jet fist pendants. They likely were not sent, but were new initiates, wanting to do something to impress their superiors. They obviously failed. But the question became, were they trying to come here to *evangelise*, or did the cult realise that the adventurers were on Patmos? After all, this time, were they still actively seeking them?

DAY 355

This is the day the ship was supposed to arrive, but it did not. It was supposed to arrive early in the morning, but it did not arrive until late in the night, and the Captain wanted to drink and sleep on the Island of Patmos, planning to leave the next day at noon.

DAY 356

Everything went as planned, and the ship set off for Corinth. They expected to arrive the next day unless anything unplanned were to happen. Unfortunately, the unplanned had become the norm on their trip.

DAY 359

It was late at night, three days later, when they arrived at Corinth. After docking, they headed to the inn that Vhaidra and Nikodemos had stayed at before and made plans to sleep there for the night.

CHAPTER XXVII
ENGAGING IN CONVERSION

That night, Nikodemos and Vhaidra went out to dinner by themselves. Nikodemos found a small romantic place that the innkeeper had recommended.

Vhaidra was touched by the thoughts of her Hypo. She loved them being able to finally have time together with no distractions these recent days.

"Hypo, I want to tell you something important."

"As do I."

"Ok, but please let me go first, Hypo."

"Of course, Vhaidra!" he chuckled.

"Well, I have decided to join your faith, The Way, and worship The Ancient of Days that you worship. I have seen how the Creator-Logos-Ghost has strengthened you and Elder Dionysios. I have no plans of ever leaving your side, and I would like this constant companionship to continue inside the temple as well."

"I had prayed this day would happen, Vhaidra!" he replied excitedly, giving her a kiss.

"Now, you had something important to tell me, Hypo?"

"Oh, yes, you almost made me forget," he said with a wink.

Nikodemos got down on one knee, as violists and cellists came around the table and started to play beautiful music. He opened a box with a rolling ring. Each of the three interconnected rings was made of bone and highly polished. He announced, "Vhaidra, you have made me the happiest man in the world. You are the greatest treasure that this world could offer me, a treasure that I am completely unworthy of. But still, I dare ask to become even luckier by becoming your husband, until death do us part. Vhaidra, the one true love of my life, will you marry me?"

Marriage was something completely alien to a drow, as was monogamy. But since she had been studying Hypo on her own, then learning overworld customs from Ti'erra, and most recently, religious teachings from Elder Dionysios, she had come to accept the concept. But to accept it for herself was something else, something much deeper. But, she could think of no one she would rather spend the rest of his life with, even though she would likely live much longer than him. So, she also got on her knees and whispered, "Yes, yes, I will marry you, Hypo." with tears rolling out of her eyes.

She hugged him and held him tighter than ever, possibly bruising one of his ribs in the process. He blotted her eyes and put the ring on her hand. She loved that he got her bone rings rather than metal with her rust monster phobia. She kept looking at it and then at him, her eyes remaining misty.

Their food came, and they finished their meal, before walking home hand-in-hand. They announced their plans to the elder, who was pleased. Nikodemos found it hard to sleep that night, not only due to his rib injury, but he was also so very happy about his future, but quite fearful that they may not survive tomorrow's battle. The rolling ring was something Nikodemos had got a monk to craft while they were staying at the Monastery of Agiou Ioanni Theologou on Patmos. Vhaidra thought it was the most beautiful thing she had ever seen. Ti'erra noticed her friend's misty eyes and new ring and screamed with delight, "Monk, did he... did he... did he?"

"Yes, Ti'erra, he asked me to be his wife!" she replied.

Ti'erra squealed with delight and hugged her friend, "You two are going to make such beautiful babies!"

Vhaidra hadn't thought about that, but now, she thought her friend was probably right. But also, these babies would probably be bigger than normal drow babies, so she might find more pain in this than most. This worried her, but she also knew that she has dealt with any pain this world had thrown at her so far.

CHAPTER XXVIII
IT'S THE FINAL COUNTDOWN

DAY 360

The team thought it best to arrive in Sicyon after dark, to be more anonymous. So, during the day, they practised battle techniques at half-speed to prepare without wearing themselves out. Vhaidra set up a plan of how to defend and then attack. They were not sure how many people they would be facing, but their intel made it likely that there were at least one hundred men in the Jet Fist Cult who would likely have either clubs, staffs, swords, or daggers on them. The most dangerous would be Zyx'Vuts, the acolyte of five evil deities, one for each finger of his hand. It could be far worse if he called down Lord Kajne the Jet Fist God, but thankfully, the evil God was not one to come out from the shadows, but rather give his power and responsibility to his chosen.

Vhaidra explained it as such, "Zyx'Vuts is an acolyte of five deities, so he is very powerful. But as jealous as most Gods are I think he will only be able to call down the power of Lord Kajne when we meet with him. So, while he may be a 'chosen' of Lord Kajne, we have the 'chosen' of The Ancient of Days. So, we have an advantage there."

"Monk, who is the 'chosen' of The Ancient of Days? The wizard?" Ti'erra asked.

"No, Hypo is," she replied matter-of-the-factly.

Nikodemos was surprised to hear her say this. Yes, he was able to wear the Armour of The Ancient of Days, but it had been lost; clearly, he was not the 'chosen.' "Who told you this, Vhaidra?" he asked.

"The Dark Maiden told me in her temple. She said in another time or place, I could have been her 'chosen,' but you are the 'chosen' of The Ancient of Days, and for me to follow you and the Creator-Logos-Ghost, as this was my true destiny."

Nikodemos' mouth was agape, and all he could say was, "Wow!"

"Anyway, as I was saying, we have that possible advantage, but first, we will have to get all his minions. Most will not be trained fighters, but some will be. If possible, I think it is wisest to focus on the trained warriors first, as they can do the most damage to us."

"I agree, Vhaidra. In fact, some of the commoners may be under the control of Zyx'Vuts, and not be following Lord Kajne of their own free will," concurred Elder Dionysios.

"That may be, but some of them may have to die so that we may live," Vhaidra retorted

"I propose that once we get into Sicyon, we head straight to the monastery so that we can get Mikhail and Miriam to safety before the fight begins," the elder suggested.

"That is not a bad plan, Elder Dionysios, but the fight may begin as soon as we get to the city's gate."

"There may be a battle there, but I think we can make it there before the war starts."

"Ok, I have an idea. I think that the best thing to do is to call down your thunderclouds once we enter and then, I will start my darkness spell, hiding us in a black cloud among the thunderclouds. The clouds would give us coverage until we get to the monastery's orphanage."

"Good plan, Vhaidra!" Nikodemos interrupted.

"Then, once we drop off Mikhail and Miriam, we run to the city's centre, circling around the fountain, so no one can attack us from behind."

During the day, the group rested in shifts and prepared to venture to Sicyon once nightfall was upon them. They knew there were Jet Fist Cult members in Corinth previously, and that they may have been watched.

That night, Elder Dionysios and Hypodiakonos Nikodemos led the group to visit Episkopos Grigorios, asking him for a blessing. There, they heard the horrible news.

"Word has travelled to us that the Jet Fist Cult has grown erratic and destroyed our temple and all the other temples in Sicyon. Last we heard, Episkopos Chrysostom and the other clergy were holed up at the *Transfiguration Cenobium.*"

"Then, we must go there at once!" Nikodemos sternly stated.

"May The Ancient of Days preserve the souls of his saints." Episkopos Grigorios said, blessing them.

"He guards the paths of justice and preserves The Way of his saints," Nikodemos replied.

The episkopos concluded, "Let the high praises of The Ancient of Days be in their mouth, and a two-edged sword in their hand; to execute vengeance upon the heathen, and punishments upon the people; to bind their kings with chains, and their nobles with fetters of iron; to execute upon them the judgement written: this honour have all his saints. Praise ye, the Creator-Logos-Ghost."

They all replied, "Amin," and kissed the episkopos' hand, even Ti'erra.

Vhaidra waited until they were out of town, and then, called Skeletogre to rise as they headed towards Sicyon.

CHAPTER XXIX
ENTER INTO CERTAIN DEATH

DAY 361

It was after midnight when they reached Sicyon. Elder Dionysios started to chant for thunderclouds to appear as they approached one of the more minor entrances. As expected, there were guards when they tried to enter. Unfortunately, the four guards recognised them.

"You are the ones wanted by the Jet Fists for stealing their property!"

"And they have brought me back," Ti'erra quipped.

"That will not be enough; there are consequences for theft and interest due in addition to the lost profits."

"How is this for interest?" Vhaidra asked, throwing daggers at all four guards. Nikodemos sliced one guard in half, and Ti'erra pounded another one unconscious. Skeletogre stabbed the third, and surprising everyone, Miriam shot a quiver of arrows into the fourth guard's face.

"Vicious ranger skills, Milkmaid!" Ti'erra giggled.

"Whatever it takes to protect my people of The Way," Miriam sternly replied.

The clouds rolled in, and Vhaidra collected her daggers while calling for a sphere of darkness to conceal them. They headed for the monastery and thankfully, entered undetected.

When they arrived, they found Episkopos Chrysostom. He was glad to see them. He had hopes that they would be able to save the city from the evil cult.

Seeing Miriam, he handed her a note, saying, "I am so sorry."

Miriam burst into tears, telling the others that the Jet Fist Cult had learned of her assistance to these so-called *criminals*, and as such, they assassinated her husband, her mother, and her father, and then sent a note to the episkopos of Sicyon to ensure Miriam found out.

Elder Dionysios apologised for getting her involved.

"I do not blame you, Elder, I only blame the damned heretical cult. Kill them all in the name of my beloved husband, mother, and father, please. Protect The Way!"

"We will, Miriam, we will. I promise you!" Vhaidra replied, holding the human female, trying to comfort her.

Episkopos Chrysostom asked, "Did you enter unseen?"

"I think so," the elder replied.

"Good, then our Hypodiakonos Nikodemos can assist at Orthros and Liturgy. Then, rest before you confront the Jet Fist Cult. I have missed his assistance in the life of The Way."

Vhaidra protested, "But we had battle plans to immediately go to the fountain..."

"No, Vhaidra! I believe this is the Will of The Ancient of Days," the elder interrupted.

After the Liturgy, the episkopos asked the group to bring their weapons to the courtyard. They did, including Miriam, and he blessed them first with holy water, and then holy oil, saying, "O Ancient of Days, our Creator-Logos-Ghost, the God of power and might, powerful in strength, strong in battle, You once gave miraculous strength to Your child, Dewod, granting him victory over his opponent, the blasphemer Metaikhmion. Mercifully accept our humble prayer. Send Your heavenly blessing upon these weapons, these throwing daggers, this Yan Yue Dao, this greathammer, this Budding Staff of Harun, these twin scimitars, this bow and these arrows. Give to them power and strength that they may protect Your Holy Church, the poor and the widows, and Your holy inheritance on earth, and make them horrible and terrible to any enemy army, and grant victory to Your people for your glory, for You are our strength and protection and unto You do we send up praise and glory, to The Ancient of Days; the Creator-Logos-Ghost, now and ever, and to the ages of ages. Amin."

"Amin," they all replied.

"Why did you bring your weapons, Milkmaid?" Ti'erra asked.

Miriam butted in, "I am not staying behind."

"What?" everyone asked.

"I am going with you; I could never forgive myself if something happened to all of you because I did not fight at your side. I've already lost my family to this cult."

"What about Mikhail?" Nikodemos added.

"There are plenty of milkmaids in the orphanage," she explained.

"But you have no armour, Milkmaid!" added Ti'erra.

"No, but maybe, we can get some for me?"

Vhaidra thought, and then, she realised that she still had the cloak that she had taken from the dead drow priestess. She took it out and looked at it carefully. Yes, this would fit Miriam. It would only go down to her mid-thigh, but it could help.

"Miriam, this is a drow priestess' *cape of invisibility*. It is soft as silk, but it also protects like iron. It will only cover your torso, but it is some protection from the eyes of the cult," Vhaidra explained.

Ti'erra offered her the copper dragon scale armour bracers and boots as well, as it would give her some protection with the tall arm-length bracers and thigh-high boots to protect her arms and legs. She had thankfully not given these items to the obsidian dragon mother of Mikhail who had been posing as a high elf, so she still had them. Ti'erra decided from now on, she would call Miriam, '*Ranger*' instead of 'Milkmaid,' since this was her new role for their upcoming battle.

Nikodemos, seeing his marks begin to glow again, against Vhaidra's protests, offered up his red dragon scale armour.

"Thank you all, I will wear them, but maybe, modify them. May The Ancient of Days be with us all."

"Amin," they all replied.

The episkopos responded, "But first, you eat dinner. At three P.M. tomorrow, the Jet Fist Cult will meet at the statue of Lord Kajne in the middle of town. While you fight, I will be in the *temple,* praying for you along with the *presvyteroi, diakonoi,* and all of the monks of The Way."

Everyone was nervous, but they knew they needed to be prepared for this battle. So, they had a great meal full of foods known to give great strength and constitution. Before they left, the elder spoke to the episkopos about Vhaidra's desire to convert, and Nikodemos' desire to marry her. Because of this, before they left the monastery, he made her a katichoumenos, giving her right to burial as a member of The Way if she died. They also did the service of the *aravones,* making the couple officially *betrothed* to one another. This required all of the *responsibilities* of *marriage,* with none of the marital *rights.*

That night supper was silent, as was the monastic tradition, each person trying to think of what the next day would bring.

CHAPTER XXX
THIS WILL BE THE END OF THEM

DAY 362

That morning, everyone was shocked when Miriam appeared wearing a red dragon scale armour dress, with the drow priestess' cape of invisibility turned into a full-body slip under it. She also had the copper dragon scale bracers, boots and had a headdress over her long brown wavy hair.

"What did you do?" cried out a visibly irritated Vhaidra.

"I put the cloak of *invincibility* under the armour as an added layer of protection and softness," Miriam explained.

"No, it was a cloak of invisibility! It makes you invisible!" Vhaidra noted, "Now that you wear it under the armour, it is useless."

"I'm sorry, I don't understand. It still protects like iron, right?"

Nikodemos butted in, "Vhaidra is saying *invisibility*; you are saying *invincibility*!"

"Oh my! I am so sorry, Vhaidra, I misunderstood you due to your accent. Please forgive me."

Vhaidra walked away, upset and mumbling to herself.

"I said I was sorry...," Miriam repeated.

At the next liturgy, the episkopos asked if anyone had any reason that he should not marry Nikodemos and Vhaidra. He would do this for three days before he could marry them. One person spoke up and mentioned that she was not a full member of The Way yet. The episkopos explained that she would receive the full *initiation mysteries* in two days. He wanted her to be a katichoumenos for three days before receiving her into The Way. No one else objected. He then anointed Elder Dionysios, Hypodiakonos Nikodemos and Miriam with the *efchelaio*, which was spiritual preparation for healing or death for full members of The Way.

During the day, Nikodemos collected as many healing potions as he could, mixed them with pain-numbing potions and energy potions, and put them in a bag of holding. If damaged badly, they would need to heal, but to keep fighting until the end, they would need to not feel the pain and also be full of energy.

Everyone was solemn as they left the monastery when it came near to three P.M. They had come up with a plan and hoped it would work. First, they marched up to the statue, which was surrounded by a small pool of water. Next, Elder Dionysios used his chant and levitated them so that they stood on top of the statue of Lord Kajne. Nikodemos put his bag of healing potions over the shoulder of the jet-black Lord Kajne statue.

The local crowd gasped, shocked at such blasphemous actions towards Lord Kajne's statue. Vhaidra yelled out, "You seek us and kill innocents because you say we stole your 'property.' Well now, we are here with your self-proclaimed *property,* and we dare to tell you that she is not *property* but rather *our friend* and belongs to no one but herself!"

There were four roads connecting to the city centre. From the north road, came a booming voice, "Nice speech, Drow, but all of these people are my property, and you can either submit to me as your master, or you can die."

The voice belonged to Zyx'Vuts, the high elf acolyte of Lord Kajne and four other evil Gods. He was clad in yellowish earth-tone robes and wore on his left hand a solitary *enchanted jet gauntlet*, which he held in a fist pointing to the six adventurers.

"How about a third choice, Acolyte? We kill you!" Ti'erra dared to shout back.

"I dare you to do your best, half-elf! Jet Fists, attack!" he screamed, sticking his thumb out to the ground on his enchanted jet gauntlet on his right hand.

They expected the Jet Fists of the statue to attack them, but this did not happen. Instead, about one hundred cult members headed at them from each of the four cardinal directions, much more than they anticipated. So, they split up. Nikodemos took the north, Vhaidra and Skeletogre to the east, Elder Dionysios took the south, while Ti'erra and Miriam pointed their eyes to the west.

Vhaidra cried out, "No time to separate the skilled from the unskilled. Kill them all!"

The Jet Fists rushed the statue on which the heroes were perched. Nikodemos was swinging his Yan Yue Dao like a madman in vertical circles over his head as he ducked down. He sliced and threw off dozens of commoner followers left, right, forward, and backwards. As if there was ever any doubt, he would never be a full diakonos or presbyteros now.

Vhaidra shot a cloud of acid into the middle of the legion headed towards her, then she jumped from the statue and started whipping her hair along with punching and kicking, killing, and knocking unconscious one person after another. Meanwhile, Skeletogre was using his twin diamond scimitars to swing back and forth, slicing and dicing cultists all around him.

Elder Dionysios called for a great earthquake to extend out in front of him, and the street broke open, swallowing up all one hundred of the cultists headed towards him.

Ti'erra wandered out into the swarm of men approaching her position, swinging her greathammer in a circle like she was doing a hammer throw. Miriam stayed up upon the jet statue and fired arrows at the approaching cultists.

Once the majority of the cultists had been incapacitated or killed, Zyx'Vuts screamed, pointing his first finger out, "*Shi Jin Generals* of the North Winter, East Spring, South Summer, and West Autumn, attack!"

From the north appeared a female drow warrior with pitch-black skin, wearing giant tortoise shell armour and carrying a single-headed snake whip of a low house drow priestess. How she could wield such a weapon, not being a priestess, was unknown to Vhaidra.

'*She must be a wielder of very powerful magicks,*' she thought to herself.

From the east appeared an albino tiger-man, wearing iron scale armour decorated with a unicorn horn on his helmet. He held an iron greatsword and had a fisheye designed shield that was tied to one of his iron gauntlets.

From the south appeared a red phoenix-like man, an *alkonost*, flying in the sky as there was no longer a road to walk on, holding a group of fiery spears in his foot-claws.

From the west appeared a half-dragon who looked more dragon-like than any half-dragon they had ever seen before. He looked just like a green dragon in humanoid body shape but a dragon-shaped head and tail, wearing a blue robe and holding an azure magickal wooden staff. "Hey, dragon, you want a piece of me?" Ti'erra shouted, walking towards it and stripping off all of her clothes, while dragging her hammer behind her. While she did this, Miriam shot a quiver of arrows high into the sky at an angle so that they would come down upon the half-dragon that was distracted by the alluring naked dwelf.

Elder Dionysios chanted for dark storm clouds to appear above the alkonost which started to build up electrical energy. Skeletogre charged towards the albino tiger-man.

Nikodemos took a deep breath and charged towards the dark elf warrior. The drow warrior had other plans and chanted something and blew air out of her pursed lips, freezing him in a solid block of ice.

Seeing this, Vhaidra went over behind her frozen Hypo, trying to stay out of sight of the drow general. She used her daggers as ice picks, to remove him from the ice block as the dark elf warrior slowly and methodically approached, cracking her single snake whip.

The half-dragon general looked up in the sky and saw the arrows before they hit him and blew out an acrid smoke, which disintegrated the arrows. He looked down at the now naked dwelf with a mixture of anger and lust just in time to get hit in the jaw with her greathammer. The half-dragon was knocked out cold, so Ti'erra stole its beautiful azure wooden staff as a souvenir. She felt powerful magicks running through it as she hit the half-dragon with it over and over again. Seeing this, Miriam turned and fired arrows in another direction.

The alkonost general started to throw his fiery spears down at the elder, who was able to deflect most of them with his Budding Rod of Harun. Unfortunately, he did end up taking a spear to his left foot along with some that simply pinned him, via his robe, to the statue, catching his robe on fire.

The tiger-man general had to dodge another volley of arrows that came in his direction, and in doing so, he leapt onto Skeletogre and ripped him to shreds, only getting minor flesh wounds in return. Skeletogre was simply no match for this wild beast-man.

Within moments, thunder and lightning strikes crashed down upon the alkonost, rendering it unable to fly, falling into the pit where the street used to be. The rain came down with such ferocity that it shortly put the fire out on the elder's robes. However, the white cloth sewn-in markings on Dionysios' robe were gone, replaced by dark black marks, where the sun had never touched. One could still see the symbols that were once sewn into the robe with white cloth pieces, over the greyed robe; it appeared that the dark-grey robe itself had been rather flame-retardant, just not the white cloth strips. Unfortunately, the elder's face, hands, and feet had been burned, causing him pain. But he tried to push through.

Vhaidra was unaware of what had happened to Skeletogre since she was so singularly focused on trying to get her Hypo out of the block of ice that thankfully was now also beginning to melt due to the pouring rain.

The tiger general then pounced upon his attacker on top of the statue. Miriam was able to grab an arrow and pierce his heart with it, but unfortunately, she could not keep her grip on the soaking wet jet statue, so she slipped and fell, hitting the back of her head on the base of the statue with a nasty cracking sound. She did not move, but lay motionless in the water, with her eyes wide open. The elder had tried to catch her but was unable to with the spears in his foot and robes, mounting him to the base of the statue.

Vhaidra was finally able to get most of the ice off her Hypo, but he was still seemingly frozen inside. The drow general flicked her whip at him, and the snake bit his arm, but it could not penetrate past his skin. This confused the general, but what happened next caused even more confusion. From behind Nikodemos, Vhaidra grabbed the snake whip and pulled hard, making the dark elf warrior general come face-to-face with Nikodemos. Then, Vhaidra flipped from behind the cleric to behind the general, grabbing her hair to make her look at the sky, while she quickly cut her throat open, saying, "Surprise, witch!"

Vhaidra decapitated the head of the snake whip and then screamed, "I need healing potions, *NOW*!" as she sucked the poison out of the snake whip bite before spitting in the head of the drow general that she held in her hand. Humans were quite susceptible to poison, unfortunately.

Ti'erra looked back. She and Vhaidra were the only ones functional. Getting potions was going to be up to her. She ran back, naked as the day that she was born, holding the stolen azure wooden staff and her greathammer in her hands. Using the staff, she grabbed the bag from the statue and passed out healing potions first to the wizard and then to the monk. The dwelf then put the staff down so that she could use her greathammer to break the spear that had pinned his foot to the base of the statue.

Elder Dionysios screamed out in pain, and Zyx'Vuts laughed. The elder took off his robe to dislodge it from the statue, briefly being completely naked, to the dwelf's delight, and then, he put it back on, the holes mysteriously mending themselves.

Next, the evil acolyte chanted, sticking out his middle finger towards the sky and made all of the dead Jet Fist Cult members and dead generals rise as undead warriors. Luckily for the party of six, many of the original commoners had not died but were just wounded or knocked out, so they did not have a full one hundred undead to face in each direction.

As the thunderclouds began to fade away, Elder Dionysios chanted and closed the ground that had been opened by his earthquake, sealing the south direction of any undead, including the alkonost general, who had fallen into the pit when he was electrocuted by the many bolts of lightning.

Vhaidra still had a hold of the drow general's hair and neck, so she twisted the neck three hundred and sixty degrees and broke her head right off. Then, she kicked the body into the water around the statue. She then got a wicked smile on her face as used the head of the drow general as a *flail* along with her martial arts skills to break the bones of the undead creatures to the north while she chanted and raised Skeletogre back up, who put down the undead villains to the east with his enchanted diamond scimitars.

Nikodemos came-to slowly, but he was very cold and could not move easily. He could just crack a smile to see Vhaidra taking the flank he was assigned to. He began chanting a circle of healing to try and somewhat heal himself, Elder Dionysios, and Miriam. Through his healing chant, he could tell that this was not going to work on Miriam, as she was now reposed. Her *angel* was already escorting her soul to the afterlife.

Ti'erra had dropped off the azure wooden staff near the elder and then, returned to her flank and had fun freezing and breaking the undead with her great enchanted hammer. In the process, she found her clothes so that she could put them back on, as not to distract any of her party. She knew that the monk would not be happy if she continued to prance around in the nude in front of the cleric that she was now engaged to.

The now undead tiger general was charging and about to spear Elder Dionysios with his unicorn helmet just as the Uncreated Light came down at the command of Dionysios' chant, killing all the undead monsters and the undead people after a howling mass scream. The elder then collapsed in pain and exhaustion, holding the helmet that had come so close to piercing his heart. Zyx'Vuts hissed and pointed his ring finger, full of enchanted rings, at the jet statue of Lord Kajne, which then suddenly came alive.

The statue eyed the now-dead Miriam and stepped on her, crushing her thighs while he laughed. The elder screamed out and grabbed the azure staff in addition to his Budding Staff to hit the statue. Neither did any good. Instead, he found himself kicked into the water surrounding the statue. Lord Kajne's statue then went to step on him too, but Dionysios used the two staffs to prevent himself from being crushed too badly. However, he was now pinned underwater and would quickly drown if he could not find a way to escape. While underwater, he started to chant.

Above water, Ti'erra had fully dressed and ran to his rescue, hitting the leg out from under the living statue, making it fall face-first into the water. The elder found himself now face-to-face with the jet statue as he finished his chant, turning the water into living blood, which held the statue of Lord Kajne's head and hands in the water while Ti'erra continued to break its lower body into pieces with her greathammer.

Dionysios came out of the living blood, the black of his robes stained blood red, and stood with Ti'erra and the returning Vhaidra and Skeletogre, along with a slowly thawing Nikodemos. "I hope that is all he has. I don't think we can take anymore," he exhaustedly sputtered.

Zyx'Vuts raised his pinky finger to the side and appeared to split into four, each one of his four bodies standing at the four cardinal directions that the legendary generals had come from. All four of him charged towards the city square's centre, where the statue once had stood.

The elder collapsed again while weakly chanting. When the four versions of the acolyte arrived, the elder continued to chant again in a strained voice, while pulling himself up, using the two staffs as support, "The kingdom of the Ten Heavens is at hand. Heal the sick, cleanse the lepers, raise the dead, cast out the devils, freely you have received, freely you shall give." He fell back to his knees and pointed his staffs and energy came pulsating out of them towards the five other members of his party.

Nikodemos could do almost nothing, as one of the four Zyx'Vutses started hitting him with a sword at a stupendous pace. But, with every hit, the marks in the hypodiakonos' skin glowed brighter, and he realised he was feeling no pain from the sword attacks even though he was bleeding from the cuts. He also felt infused with energy. With renewed strength and absolute confirmation of his internalisation of the Armour of The Ancient of Days, he grabbed the shoulders of the high elf acolyte, spun him around, and head-butted him in the nose, causing this Zyx'Vuts to fall backwards into the living blood, which began to drown him too.

Vhaidra was able to grab one of the Zyx'Vutses from behind, holding his arms to his sides, and tripped him with her legs, causing him to land on his face, breaking his nose and orbital socket, rendering him unconscious. In the process, however, the half-high elf acolyte successfully cut her thigh with a nasty gash to the bone that poured out blood at a deadly rate, as it had severed an artery. She knew she had to stab him with her daggers quickly, and thankfully, she was able to.

Ti'erra tried to hit the third Zyx'Vuts with her greathammer as she danced, but he was too fast. He began to laugh at her as she tried even harder to hit him but failed. But the laughter stopped suddenly when he found twin scimitars sticking through his chest from behind, courtesy of the forgotten Skeletogre, who Vhaidra had raised yet again as she bled out.

The fourth Zyx'Vuts quickly approached the elder, who was still on his knees, and he happily found a victim that could not fight back. Dionysios simply said, "Greater love has no man than this, that a man lays down his life for his friends." and stretched his arms out while raising his chin, ready to die. Zyx'Vuts swung his sword mightily, but before he could finish his slice, he found an arrow coming through his heart from behind. Looking back, he saw a resurrected, de-aged, and healed female human ranger that looked to be about sixteen years of age, with bow and arrow in hands.

"Thank you, Elder Dionysios," she added, her voice a little higher pitched than before and full of vitality.

"No, thank *you*, Miriam!" he replied. His chant had worked, and just in the nick of time!

Energy shot from the four Zyx'Vuts bodies and came together over where the statue used to stand and the four now dead or dying bodies combined. Zyx'Vuts then circled himself in necromancy and used the power of his multiple deaths to power himself up, and in the process, became a completely undead being himself, shedding his hair, skin, muscle, and his mortal coil. But he was not just any undead being; he still had a beating jet heart, shaped not unlike a fist that powered his necromancy. The black heart absorbed the power of death from all the dead beings around them and glowed an eerie black glow. He floated down to the base of the now-destroyed statue and laughed an insane laugh so loud that everyone's ears began to bleed.

Angrily, he smashed his left fist into the ground, breaking the enchanted jet gauntlet of Lord Kajne and shooting power down into the *nine hells* as he called on four-hundred demons to arise from the lower *demonic pits* and attack the group. That would mean sixty-six point six demons would go against each of the six party members.

"Surely, we will die today!" Vhaidra sighed and kissed her Hypo, knowing this battle would be over in moments. She could take on several demons and perhaps live if she was lucky and not bleeding profusely from her leg, but sixty-six point six were impossible for anyone. She hoped to enter the *shades* with her beloved at her side at least.

"Then, let us make it a good death," Nikodemos replied, readying his weapon with his newfound vigour, as the demons leapt up, ready to rain down on their prey and reign over the city after their death.

Ti'erra could not do anything other than open her mouth and say, "Fuuuuuuuuhhhhhhh..."

During all of this, Elder Dionysios, with great effort, chanted, "Thus shall it be in the consummation of the age; the angels shall go forth, and shall separate the evil from the midst of the righteous, and shall cast them into the furnace of fire. There shall there be the weeping and the gnashing of the teeth." Once he completed the chant, a trumpet blasted from the heavens. Four Archangels, Zadkiel-Jeremiel, Barachiel-Jophiel, Raguel-Jehudiel, and Camael-Salathiel, descended from the ten heavens while four other Archangels arrived from the four cardinal directions. Each of the eight Archangels led an army of fifty angels apiece. One hundred other angels raced from the monastery to join the battle along with three additional angels, one assigned for each Dionysios, Nikodemos, and Miriam as their *guardians*. As full members of The Way, they each had *guardian angels* assigned to them specifically to help them fight demons.

Vhaidra was right; the battle ended quickly. Time seemed to stop as the demons descended down upon them. The angels, however, took out the demons in what seemed to only be an instant, but was much more, as it was actually a very long battle, fought outside of time, destroying the demons' power and locking them back away in the nine hells. The angels and Archangels then returned to the ten heavens before Zyx'Vuts knew what happened.

Nikodemos ran at Zyx'Vuts and splashed him with holy water and pierced Zyx'Vuts' dark heart with his jade Yan Yue Dao. He then flung the undead body at Ti'erra, screaming, "Hammer time!"

The dwelf hit Zyx'Vuts' skull with all her might, cracking it in half and knocking his body to Skeletogre, who stuck his scimitars into the evil being's hip sockets, shattering them. Vhaidra used a trick she had learned in the monasteries and hopped over to the elder, grabbing the azure staff and used it to launch herself in the air like a pole vaulter. In the air, she raised the staff over her head, then she landed, she brought the staff down with both hands and with such force that it splintered Zyx'Vuts' bones as well as the azure staff into many pieces. She was sad that this staff was not unbreakable like the one that she had owned in the underworld. The magickal explosion from the destruction of the magick-filled azure wooden staff gave her one thousand tiny cuts that were instantly cauterised by the magickal explosion, and the force of the explosion threw her into Hypo's arms, where she was happy to stay. She began to chant as she became sleepy from the loss of blood from her leg.

Miriam then gathered the pieces of the bones, placed them at the base of the destroyed statue, and poured holy salt on them, which made a horrible hissing sound. Vhaidra finished her chant for a cloud of acid while the elder called down the fireballs, destroying all that was left of the acolyte's undead body.

Then, there was a silence that was not only caused by the bleeding of their eardrums. The heroes looked around at one another, wondering if it was really over. It truly was! It was finally over! They had impossibly destroyed the Jet Fist Cult and Lord Kajne's acolyte. They would live to see another day!

There were hugs all around until the newly young Miriam's voice rang out, "Stand still!" The team looked at her and saw she had the bow loaded with an arrow. "Don't move!" she ordered as she fired arrow after arrow at them.

The arrows went whizzing between their heads, arms, torsos, and in between their legs as Miriam kept firing. When she stopped, they looked around to see an approaching half-dragon full of arrows falling to the ground, dead.

"You don't even want to know what I was thinking, Ranger!" laughed Ti'erra. Miriam smiled and laughed with her as they helped the elder to the monastery. Nikodemos ran, carrying his Vhaidra, who had ordered Skeletogre to clean up the mess in the streets with the last of her breath before she lost consciousness.

Tierra came back quickly and claimed the downed drow's giant tortoise armour for herself, finding it beautiful.

CHAPTER XXXI
REST IN PEACE

Back at the monastery, the female monastics took care of the adventurers' wounds and helped heal them. After being treated for their injuries and bathing, they ate a huge meal and then went to sleep for the night.

Outside, the episkopos and his fellow clerics hired a team of the laity to remove the dead bodies from the city streets by horse-drawn carts to a graveyard outside the city. Those that were found to still be alive were collected and taken to a private apothecary to be healed and then turned over to the royal authorities.

DAY 363

The next day, during the liturgy, the episkopos asked again if anyone had any reason that Nikodemos and Vhaidra should not be married. There were no reasons given, even though she was unable to be present due to her injuries.

After the Liturgy, while Vhaidra was continuing to be treated by the apothecary, Nikodemos went to look at his old home, to see if he could take up residence there again. Unfortunately, he found that it had been destroyed by the Jet Fist Cult and he would have to find another residence or build a new property on his land.

As he was out and about, he was given many gifts by those happy to see the Jet Fist Cult destroyed. He received so many gifts that he ended up buying a bag to put all of the treasures in. He carried the bag around town while he searched for homes for sale.

Archon Justinian of Sicyon approached, and Nikodemos bowed to him. Surprisingly, the archon came up to the hypodiakonos, laid his hand on his shoulder, and said, "Thank you, Nikodemos! You and your friends have saved Sicyon from the vile Jet Fist Cult!"

"It was simply our duty to our friends in this city," he replied.

"I heard the cult destroyed your home."

"Yes, yes, this is true. But how did you know, sir?"

"It is my job to know everything that happens in my city!"

"Of course, sir."

"If you will allow me to take your land as my own, I will give you my seventh home just outside the city gates in exchange."

"*Omorfia Dipla Sto Potami*?" he asked, knowing the name of the famous home that they had passed when leaving the city almost a year ago.

"Yes, I see you know of it."

"We all do, sir, but it is too much."

"Then, consider it a wedding gift and your former home will be considered a payment for the destruction the city saw yesterday."

"Yes, sir," he bowed, submitting to the will of the archon.

"We will speak of this battle another day, Nikodemos, but you may take up residency in two days," and with that, the archon's servant gave him the keys and continued on to the city centre.

Nikodemos decided that he would not talk to Vhaidra about this until after they married.

DAY 364

The next day, the Episkopos asked for the third time if anyone had any reason that Nikodemos and Vhaidra should not be married. Again, there were no reasons given. Vhaidra was glad that followers of The Way were not racist against her like so many others in the overworld. The healing clerics at the monastery were doing great work on her leg and other wounds. While Vhaidra would have a lifelong scar from her thigh wound, she was able to walk and would receive the initiation mysteries of a member of The Way today. Miriam acted as her *nouna* or sponsor. She said it was the least that she could do, since being de-aged, she no longer could be a milkmaid for Mikhail or any of the other children in the orphanage.

Vhaidra did not ever remember wearing all white as she did today for the initiation rites of entering into The Way. It was a white cowled and closed robe with the Symbol of The Way on the back of the garment in red and at the front of the cowl. She would wear all white again tomorrow as was the custom of overworlders to do this for a wedding. She envied Hypo that he could wear his regular white robe while she would be wearing a white dress made by Miriam. While her Hypo told her that she looked wonderful in white, she was not sure. She preferred the black leather clothes that she had worn every day since her youth as a monk.

DAY 365

After the wedding, they had a huge feast where Vhaidra heard all of Nikodemos' friends, whom she was meeting for the first time, call him "Demos." It was interesting. She called him Hypo, and the clerics all called him Nikodemos, Ti'erra called him "Cleric," and his friends called him Demos. Also interesting was that his house or family name, which he rarely had ever used with her in conversation, had legally become hers as well, so she was now known as Vhaidra Iroas, or Mrs. Iroas, in the overworld. When she returned to the underworld, having no drow house in her heart and mind, she would call herself Vhaidra of House Iroas. But first, she was going to raise up a powerful house in the overworld!

After the feast and ritual dance, they had a wedding march to their new home, followed by all the guests. Vhaidra was surprised. It was such a marvellous castle made of dark-grey stone. She would need to redecorate, removing all of the metal, but it was a beautiful home, the inside of which was not unlike one that would belong to a great house in the underworld which had all of the magicks stripped away.

It was the day of their wedding, the day before Hypo's thirty-fourth birthday, and the day before the anniversary of the couple's first meeting. It seemed so long ago and yet, it seemed like it was yesterday in many senses. Vhaidra could not believe how much she had grown over the last year. A year was such a short amount of time for her, but she had changed more in the last year than in all the other years of her life since she joined the monastery. Not only did she live in the overworld, not only did she no longer associate with any Drow, not only was she no longer a follower of the Dark Mother, but she was also a member of The Way, a worshipper of The Ancient of Days and the bride of the luckiest bridegroom in the world, Hypo... Hypodiakonos Nikodemos, who had obtained for them a beautiful castle beside the river.

She hoped that this was not just a dream, because she could remember it just like it was yesterday...

EPILOGUE
THE END IS JUST THE BEGINNING

"Don't worry, Hypo, I am fully educated in the ways of *marital relations*, as you call them here in the overworld."

Hypodiakonos Nikodemos replied, "How? I thought you were a..."

"I am, but young drow females are allowed to watch their mother matron and were taught how to use mating activity for both pleasures of oneself, and also the pleasure or destruction of their mate."

"Destruction by mating?" Hypo excitedly asked, "I thought only *succubi* did this?"

"Succubi use mating to get a male to submit his eternal soul. Drow can use mating as a way to physically destroy a mate of prey."

"Mate of prey?"

"Don't worry, Hypo. You are not my prey," She slyly grinned.

Hypo frowned, "I am sorry to say that I am not educated in the ways of marital relations, my dear."

"Don't worry, Hypo. I will teach you!"

"That's what the succubi say!" he teased her.

"WHAT!"

"Never mind, dear," he said winking.

With that being said, she pushed him down in their marital bed and gave him a night he would never forget. A night he would also limp away from, as drow sensuality and human sensuality were not perfectly in line with one another – one of the many lessons that he learned that night.

But what happened next was a lesson that he never expected or planned for...

THE END

OF

VHAIDRA & THE DESTINY OF NIKODEMOS

To be continued in the upcoming books:

Vhaidra & the Dragon of Temple Mount

Vhaidra & the Disease of Dark Elves

Vhaidra & the Descent of House Iroas

Vhaidra & the
Demise
of House Iroas

Vhaidra & the
Dungeons
of Drow

Vhaidra & the
Demons
of Zhong

Vhaidra & the
Digest
of Short Stories

INDEX

Hierarchy of Monks

Novice: Given the black clothing of monasticism

Junior: Given the belt and headgear of monasticism

Full: Given the neckwear of monasticism

Senior: Given the armaments of monasticism

Elder: A holy enlightened senior monk

Archimandrite: Chief monk of a monastery

INDEX

Types of Monasteries

A *hermitage* is where an Elder lives in eremitic solitude rather than in a cenobitic community.

A *skete* is a small single-gender monastic establishment that usually consists of only one Elder or archimandrite and two or three disciple monks.

A *cenobium* is where many monks live together, work together, and pray together, following the directions of an archimandrite.

A *lavra* is the largest type of monastery and can hold many hundreds of monks.

INDEX

Clerical Hierarchy of The Way

Acolyte: Lights and carries both candles and incense, age 7+

Kantoros: Chants the holy hymns, age 14+

Anagnostis: Reads the holy scriptures, age 14+

Hypodiakonos: Leads acolytes & anagnostis, guards the doors, age 20+

Diakonos: Married assistant to a presbyteros and episkopos, age 25+

Ierodiakonos: Monastic assistant to a ieromonk and episkopos, age 25+

Protodiakonos: Chief diakonos of an episkopos' eparchy

Archidiakonos: Chief ierodiakonos of an episkopos' eparchy

Presbyteros: Married liturgical celebrant at a temple, age 30+

Ieromonk: Monk liturgical celebrant at a temple, age 30+

Protopresbyteros: Chief presbyteros of an episkopos' eparchy

Igumen: Chief ieromonk of an episkopos' eparchy

Episkopos: Head of all clerics in his eparchy, age 40+

Archiepiskopos: Chief episkopos of an entire nation

INDEX

Clergy Robes, Clothing, & Vestments

Monastic *clerics* wear all-black robes, vests, and hats while married *clerics* wear white robes with black vests and hats. A *hypodiakonos, kantoros, or anagnostis* that is not a monk wears a white robe like all married clergy, whether they are married or not. These three ranks of clergy are the only ranks that can marry after they are ordained. Because of this, monastic clergy are often called the black clergy, and non-monastic clergy are called the white clergy.

An *acolyte* does not wear a robe but does wear a sticharion vestment when serving

A *kantoros* does not wear vestment when serving but does wear a robe when serving

An *anagnostis* wears a robe at all times and also a sticharion vestment when serving

A *hypodiakonos* wears a robe and skufiya hat at all times, a sticharion and an orarion vestment when serving

A *diakonos* and *ierodiakonos* wears the same as a *hypodiakonos* and also cuff vestments when serving. A *protodiakonos* or *archidiakonos* wears a double orarion

A *presbyteros* and *ieromonk* wears the same as a *diakonos* and *ierodiakonos,* and also a phelonion vestment when serving. They wear their Symbol of The Way outside their robes and vestments. They are awarded the armaments of priesthood if they become a *protopresbyter* or *igumen.*

An *episkopos* wears a black robe at all times, he also wears a sticharion, a wool orarion, cuffs, and a mitre vestment when serving. He wields a double snake staff and wears an icon of the Theotokos outside their robes and vestments. An *archiepiskopos* wears both the Symbol of The Way and the Icon of the Theotokos.

INDEX

The Twelve Mysteries of The Way

Katichoumenos: a presbyteros or episkopos accepting a person to be a learner of The Way

Vaptisma: ritualistic washing in holy water by a presbyteros or episkopos

Chrisma: ritualistic anointing with holy oil by a presbyteros or episkopos

Koura: offering the first sacrifice of hair cut by a presbyteros or episkopos

Koinonia: an unknown mystery to all except full members of The Way

Exomologesis: confession of sins to The Ancient of Days overseen by a presbyteros or episkopos

Nounos/Nouna: sponsoring an initiate in entering into The Way by vaptisma

Efchelaio: ritualistic prayer for healing and preparation for death by a presbyteros or episkopos

Tafi: burial of the body of a follower of The Way by a presbyteros or episkopos

Aravones: betrothal of two followers of The Way by a presbyteros or episkopos

Gamos: marriage of two followers of The Way by a presbyteros or episkopos

Cheirothesia: ordination by laying of hands of an episkopos

INDEX

The Vhaidra Book Series

I: Vhaidra & the DESTINY of Nikodemos
Published in 2020. The *Cult of the Jet Fist* literally causes the forces of heaven and hell to collide, destroying *Sicyon* in the process. Meanwhile, the *Dark Maiden* starts drawing a line of destiny from the past to the future intersecting with the lifelines of Vhaidra and *Nikodemos*, as one house dies, and another is formed.

II: Vhaidra & the DRAGON of Temple Mount
Publishing soon. An orphaned young half-dragon, his human milkmaid, and a flirtatious dwelf dancer change the ascetic hermit, *Elder Dionysios*, forever, whether he likes it or not. *Mikhail* grows from a baby to *Sicyon's* powerful stylite and protector after the events of *VHAIDRA & the DESTINY of NIKODEMOS* and before the events of *VHAIDRA & the DISEASE of DARK ELVES.*

III: Vhaidra & the DISEASE of Dark Elves
Publishing soon. After the events of *VHAIDRA &*

the DRAGON of TEMPLE MOUNT, an *epidemic* starts to spread across *Hellas* from the *Elven lands*. As it eventually becomes a *pandemic*, it divides the city and our adventurers into *three camps*; one group blames all *elves – high, wood, and dark –* for the pandemic and starts persecuting them, another thinks it is a *false flag conspiracy* by the government to control them, and the last camp is scared to death, thinking it is a sign of it being the *last days*.

IV: Vhaidra & the DESCENT of House Iroas
Publishing soon. After the scarring events of *VHAIDRA & the DISEASE of DARK ELVES*, *Vhaidra* learns the whereabouts of the last remaining survivors of her house from the underworld just as her cold dish of *revenge* is finally ready to be served, *but at what cost?* Death finally claims many of our heroes' lives and changes the *underworld* forever. To be concluded in *VHAIDRA & the DEMISE of HOUSE IROAS*.

V: Vhaidra & the DEMISE of House Iroas
Publishing soon. A direct continuation of the story from *VHAIDRA & the DESCENT of HOUSE IROAS*. Stuck in the deepest depths of the underworld with half of our heroes now dead, the

one true *chosen one* rises from the ashes of the battle with the *Spider Queen* and saves the *overworld* from certain destruction from below! No one comes out unscathed, and no one will ever look at *House Iroas* the same way ever again!

VI: Vhaidra & the DUNGEONS of Drow
Publishing soon. What strange secrets does *Vhaidra's* long-lost indestructible staff hold, and how is it connected to the *Spider Queen?* This is the untold in-depth story of Vhaidra's conception, birth, and life in the cities and monasteries of the *underworld* of the evil *Dark Mother*, as told by Vhaidra to her eldest daughter, *Athanasia,* following the world-shattering events of *VHAIDRA & the DEMISE of HOUSE IROAS.*

VII: Vhaidra & the DEMONS of Zhong
Publishing soon. The untold in-depth story of *Nikodemos* and his introduction to the *Armour of The Ancient of Days* by Presbyteros Romanos, as told to *Vhaidra* after the shocking events of *VHAIDRA & the DEMISE of HOUSE IROAS.* We learn what really happened when he first encountered the six succubi during his journeys to the mysterious lands of the *Far East*, the *dire warning* that he receives, and

the item that he obtains which will change his *destiny* forever!

VIII: Vhaidra & the DIGEST of Short Stories
Publishing soon. A book of short stories telling the true past of Feyrdryl, Elder Dionysios, Ti'erra, Skeletogre, and many others before they met Vhaidra and Nikodemos. Is the truth stranger than what the obsidian dragon told Vhaidra about the doplegangers? Who is the true father of Ti'erra, and what was her life like as a young dwelf? What was Dionysios' life like growing up in the orphanage? Who is Dogork the Ogre, and what does his life tell us about the past life of Skeletogre before he became an undear servant? The answers to these questions and many more are answered in this exciting digest of short stories!

INDEX

About the Author

Nicholas Stanosheck, besides being an author, is a father, a world traveller, a volunteer Scout Leader, an Orthodox Christian, and a Lean Six Sigma Master Black Belt from Lincoln, Nebraska, USA who currently resides in Dallas, Texas, USA. His novels come from his lifelong love of fantasy novels, video games, world travels, and role-playing games. His first novel started as a short story that he had in his head for years, and once he committed it to write, the characters spoke to him and started telling him a series of stories about *VHAIDRA & the HOUSE of IROAS* that will continue as a paperback and e-book series for years to come. You may contact him at https://Vhaidra.com

COMING SOON
VHAIDRA & THE
DRAGON
OF TEMPLE MOUNT

Made in the USA
San Bernardino, CA
03 August 2020